The Saga of a Modern Day Lot

The Saga of a Modern Day Lot

Morris A. Matthews

TATE PUBLISHING
AND ENTERPRISES, LLC

Published by Tate Publishing & Enterprises, LLC
127 E. Trade Center Terrace | Mustang, Oklahoma 73064 USA
1.888.361.9473 | www.tatepublishing.com

Tate Publishing is committed to excellence in the publishing industry. The company reflects the philosophy established by the founders, based on Psalm 68:11,
"The Lord gave the word and great was the company of those who published it."

Book design copyright © 2016 by Tate Publishing, LLC. All rights reserved.
Cover design by Dante Rey Redido
Interior design by Gram Telen

Published in the United States of America

ISBN: 978-1-68333-735-5
1. Fiction / African American / Christian
2. Fiction / Christian / General
16.07.07

Contents

1

How Did I Get Here?

It was a Saturday in the fall in a small town in Southern Virginia. The leaves were just starting to turn colors before eventually beginning to drop to the ground. The temperature was about a breezy fifty-five degrees. It was a nice day for riding and looking at how pretty the fall season was. Hubert was about to leave his friend Donovan's house. He was going to do Donovan a favor which he thought he would forever regret. Even though Hubert had done it once before, he knew that it was wrong and he said that he would never do it again. Donovan really looked out for him the last time, financially that is. Hubert had really needed that financial help the first time and, being that he was doing it again, it seemed he needed the help once more.

"They know I'm coming, right?" asked Hubert.

"It will work out the exact same way it did last time, Huey, stop worrying, player. By this time tomorrow, we will be setting back drinking cold Coronas or Heinekens as we count all that extra change we made," said Donovan.

"I hope you're right," Hubert said very quietly.

"Look, man. Since we met haven't I always had your back?" asked Donovan.

Hubert quickly responded, "Naw, kid, I think that that is vice versa."

"Well, you're probably right," Donovan said smiling, "but did I not have your back the last time you needed me?"

"Yeah, but it was me that was taking a chance," explained Hubert.

"Yeah, I guess you are right again. But I got you this time, Hue. Now get out of here, because you are running out of time." Donovan leaned forward to shake Hubert's hand.

"I will call you when the mission is accomplished," Hubert told Donovan.

Donovan did not respond right away; he just stared into Hubert's eyes as if he were starting to get worried himself.

"Did you hear me, man?" Hubert asked.

"Huh?" said Donovan, coming out of his daze.

"I said I will call you when the mission is accomplished," repeated Hubert.

"No! Do not use the phones until I call you, okay? Whatever you do, do not forget that," answered Donovan, still seeming a little nervous. "Now you need to get on out of here, Hue."

As Hubert was beginning to get into his truck, Donovan walked over, and as he hugged him he seemed to get a little emotional saying, "Thank you for this, man, I love you, and be careful out there."

"I got this," Hubert replied. "Just don't forget to call me, because I might end up in the Bahamas somewhere sipping on gin and juice." Hubert then got into the truck, and drove off waving the peace sign.

As he pulled on to the main highway to his next destination, he drove about two and a half miles until he had to stop at the first red light. He noticed something different as he stopped. He could see several police cars up ahead as if they were about to set up a random roadblock and check for license and registration. So, Hubert, forgetting about the package he had in back of his truck, rode through the check as if he had nothing to worry about. As he approached the first police car he noticed that every officer seemed to be getting out of his or her car and getting behind their open doors. Hubert immediately went into panic mode and slammed on the brakes.

"Police," they shouted. "Get out of the truck! Get out of the truck with your hands up!" "Police. Please step out of the vehicle!"

For starters, Hubert thought that he was dreaming. He did not know what to do, but he knew that he did not want to go to jail. So he threw the truck in reverse, and began backing fast enough so that if he slammed on the brakes the truck would hopefully spin around. As he begin backing up, the police were jumping in their cars, and some were even running after him on foot, calling for backup on their radios, and yelling for him to stop, which he had no intentions of doing.

The truck did spin around as Hubert hoped that it would, so he then dumped it into drive and begin traveling back toward Donovan's house. Hubert called Donovan on his cell phone, and the phone rang and rang until the answering machine picked up. So he tried calling again, and as he passed his house he noticed that the police were already at the end of Donovan's gate as if they were expecting him to come through. The police tried to set up a roadblock, but there were only two cars, and by time they noticed Hubert he had driven right between them. So they just joined in as the chase began to grow.

Hubert figured that he could lose them by turning down Acorn Street, which is a long winding back road he knew like the back of his hand. As he started going faster he was thinking that he was getting away. Hubert looked in the mirror, and he could see one, two, three police cars following close on his trail, continuously seeming to close in as if they were chained to the back of his truck. He drove that truck like he had never driven it before, knowing that he could not get caught. He found himself passing cars, almost running them off of the road, but he wanted to get to the point where the road turned into two narrow lanes, because as a teenager he remembered being able to take the whole road at speeds of up to ninety-five miles an hour. The difference was that he was not a teenager anymore and that he was driving for his life, and he was scared to death.

As he made it to the narrow road, the police were still following close. He pushed the gas pedal down to the floor, and it appeared like he was putting a little space in between him and the police. It seemed like the faster he went the smaller the road seemed to get; and right now, he was at a point where it seemed as if he were driving through a tunnel, and the least mistake he made would land him in the hospital, or maybe worse. Right now, he could not think about that; the only thing he could think of was what he was going to do next.

He looked to be gaining more control of the truck as the roads straightened for a while, but this also seemed to help the police. Hubert started wondering what kind of engines these guys had in their cars, because he could not lose them. One police car, which was the closest to him, seemed to be just as determined to catch him as Hubert was of getting away. The officer got close enough to Hubert, and it looked like he was going to bump the back of the truck. When all of a sudden, he tried to pass on the left then tried again on the right until their vehicles rubbed one another. Hubert did not know if it scared the officer as much as it scared him, but Hubert held control of the truck. As for the officer, he ran off of the road, colliding into a tree, at a speed of over eighty miles an hour. Hubert thought to himself, *If I were to get caught, not only will I be facing felony drug charges but now even attempted murder.*

As the high-speed chase continued, the more times Hubert looked in the rearview mirror the more police cars he could see joining in, and he seemed to be running out of road. With all of the lights following, it looked like fireworks hooked on to his bumper. Still Hubert would not slow down. In a panic, and scared to death, he began to think…

He thought about how he and his little girl would always laugh and play; he thought about his mother always pushing for him to get his life straight with the church. He thought about a sermon he had heard the last time he visited church, and how the minister seemed to be talking directly to him. He thought about all the people he let down in the past, and all the people he had hurt, wondering to himself, *What made me into this person I am, and how could I just not care about other people's feelings?* Most of all, he thought, how did he really get himself into this mess?

2

The Wedding

A few years earlier. "Ladies and gentlemen, it gives me great pleasure to present to you, for the first time in public, Mr. and Mrs. Hubert Alexander."

Everyone stood and clapped as the newlyweds walked toward their designated table. As they reached the table, Hubert hugged his new bride, Shayla, telling her, "I'm not ready to share you with everyone just yet. Do you think they would get mad if we just left?"

"I'm pretty sure they are going to be a little upset, baby, and I paid entirely too much money for this dress, and my parents paid too much money for this whole thing. I don't think I will be leaving my own reception this early, so let's enjoy our spotlight time, and then go home and open our gifts later," said Shayla, as she kissed him on the nose. "I love you. Now pull my chair out so that I can sit down, please."

He did so, and proceeded to take a seat himself, but before he could sit, Adrian, the maid of honor, came over to hug him, saying, "Congratulations, Mr. and Mrs. Alexander! You guys looked so cute, when I was not crying."

"Which sounded like most of the wedding," said Shayla, reaching out for her hug. "I love you, girl. Thanks for bearing with me the last couple of months. You have truly been the best friend and the best maid of honor a woman could ever ask for, and I do not know what I would have done without you."

As they hugged, Adrian slowly pulled away still wiping her eyes. "Just take care of my baby's daddy."

Shayla with a quick response, "You know I got you, girl. And by the way, wasn't she gorgeous out there?"

Smiling, Hubert said, "Nikki was beautiful, and looked just like her daddy walking down the aisle dropping little flowers, looking at me like she wanted to cry. I thought that that was so cute.."

At the same time, Adrian and Shayla yelled, "Looked just like you!"

Adrian continued, saying, "Huey, please, my baby looked like an angel coming down that aisle, and if she looked like anybody, it was her mommy."

The three laughed as they took their seats.

Everyone continued eating, smiling, and enjoying the festivities as the time for the toast drew near.

"Donovan, you're up," said Hubert.

Taking a deep breath he looked at Hubert, saying, "I know."

Donovan then stood up, walked to the microphone, and tapped the side of his wine glass with a spoon, saying in a deep voice, "Attention, attention, everyone. May I have your attention, please."

The place quieted as he cleared his throat and began speaking.

"First of all, I would like to thank God for getting the men in the wedding party here safely from the bachelor party last night."

Barking and cheers were heard from the men at the wedding party table and from some of the guests, as Shayla stared into Hubert's face, smiling and rolling her eyes.

Donovan went on. "But that was all good, though." Looking at Hubert. "My freshman year of college, I was absolutely lost, away from home for the first time, not knowing anybody." He paused. "You know, I really did not like school, but being I had a scholarship, I chose school, because I was not going to the military. So I told myself I would try college, to see how it would go. The first day of football practice, I met a guy, cocky, crazy, confident, but could not play the least bit of football."

Everyone laughed. He grinned and looked over at Hubert as he continued.

"But he could make you think that he was the best on the field at every position, from quarterback to the punter, he could do it all. And even though he couldn't teach me much about football, I learned a lot about everything else from him. Huey, you are like the brother I never had, and I love you."

He paused again.

"At one time I thought that no one could slow you down, but along comes Shayla Mitchell."

He then looked at Shayla. "Shay, you have a good man, and from listening to him talk about you, he has the perfect woman. You guys look great together, and I wish you both all the happiness in the world and a prosperous future. God bless you both."

He held the glass up and everyone did the same.

"Oh, Adrian," Shayla called out, "your turn."

Adrian stood and looked as if she were going to start crying before she even said a word.

"I'm all right," she started. "Shay, I know that we started out on the wrong foot a few years ago, and I understood, but you have become one of the most special people in my life."

She started to cry, but continued. "You have been a sister to me, a mother to my child, and sometimes a mother to me. As Don stated, Huey would always say you are the perfect woman. I am so glad I got the chance to learn this firsthand, and I truly agree."

She stopped, holding one hand in the air, getting herself together.

Donovan told her, "Take your time, baby."

She then looked over at Hubert, and began again.

"Hubert Alexander," she said, wiping her eyes, trying to smile. "That's just my baby's daddy." The crowd laughed. "I have known you my whole life and you have never been less than an outstanding friend, a great father, and a focus-driven person. If you give that same energy to your marriage, with the same exact intensity, you two are guaranteed to grow old together. Again, congratulations and good luck at pursuing every dream you guys have together, and I wish you the best. I love you both."

She then held her glass up and everyone did the same. Hubert, Shayla, Donovan, and Adrian all shared a group hug as the guests applaud.

The reception continued on, and as Hubert and Shayla were dancing together, Hubert could feel something pulling at the bottom of his coat. He turned. It was his daughter, Monique "Nikki."

"Hi, baby," he said, picking her up in his arms. "Would you like to cut in?"

"Cut in what?" she asked, laughing.

"I'm going over and getting something to drink," Shayla said as she kissed Nikki on the forehead. "I'll be back soon. I love you, Mr. Alexander."

"I love you too, Mrs. Alexander," Hubert said as he started to dance, holding his daughter in his arms, as if she were his dancing partner.

"Daddy," Nikki said softly, "I have a question for you."

"What question do you have for me, baby?" Hubert asked Monique, smiling.

"Is Mrs. Shay going to be my new mommy?" she asked.

"Well, she is kind of, and kind of she is not," he started to explain. "See, Adrian will always be your mother, and nothing will ever change that. However, being that Mrs. Shay is now my wife, that makes her your stepmother."

"So do I call her Mrs. Step Mommy?" she asked.

Laughing, Hubert answered, "No, baby, you can still call her Mrs. Shay."

As the song came to an end, Hubert walked Nikki over to Adrian, who was talking with Shayla and Hubert's mother. His mother smiled as he gave her a great big hug.

"Congratulations, son," she said, squeezing Hubert. "You have taken another step in manhood. You have taken you a wife, and you know the Bible says that marriage is honorable. I hope that the next step is salvation. I also hope that I see the both of you in church tomorrow morning giving God the praise for allowing you two to be together. You can also come and pray to him to strengthen your relationship for the future, and just give him praise for waking you both up each and every day, because some mother is at her son's funeral right now crying, while we are here rejoicing. You need—"

"Mama!" Hubert said, interrupting her. "Come on with the sermon! We understand, we understand."

"So I hope to see you in the morning," replied Hubert's mother.

"Well, actually no," Hubert said. "We are leaving in the morning to catch a plane to San Diego."

"What's in San Diego?" questioned his mother.

"From there we are catching another plane to Hawaii, and we are staying there until Friday," explained Hubert.

"Hubert, honey, the hula is not going to get you into heaven," Hubert's mother said, pointing in his face.

"I love you, Mom," Hubert said, grabbing his mother's pointing finger and pulling her close to him for a hug.

The music that was playing had all been slow music up to that point, and then the DJ started playing a fast song, calling people to the floor to get the party started. People started grabbing others and pulling them to the floor, and soon the floor was packed as if it were a nightclub instead of a wedding reception.

Donovan came over to Hubert and his mother with a drink in his hand, bouncing up and down to the music.

"Man, this reception is banging," said Donovan. "Did you try that rum and Coke mix? Your bartender knows what he is doing, player."

"Donovan, will I see you in church tomorrow?" Hubert's mother asked.

"Mrs. Alexander, if this rum and Coke allows me to get up early enough in the morning to make it to church…" Donovan put his finger on his mouth as if in thought. "I am not even going to lie to you, ma'am, I still am not going to make it to church in the morning, but please pray for me."

Hubert's mother looked toward Donovan, then looked at Hubert, and shook her head. She then pulled Hubert closer to her and hugged him. "I have to go before I hear the people in the congregation talking about how they heard about me doing the cha-cha slide across the floor at my son's wedding reception. You know how they talk, and how they like to get things started." She paused. "Huey, you be careful on that honeymoon of yours, and I will be praying for a safe trip out there, and a safe trip back home for you, but you have to remember to do the same. God loves you, and I love you. Now I am going to find that beautiful daughter-in-law of mine, and then I am leaving. Try and call me just so I know that you made it safely out there."

"All right, Ma, I love you too," Hubert said as his mother walked away. "And, Ma, what do you know about a cha-cha slide anyway?"

Hubert's mother found Shayla, gave her a big hug, and then left the reception. Hubert and Shayla went out to the dance floor for a few songs together, and as they completed their dance Adrian came over and grabbed Shayla.

"Girl, we have not taken a picture together yet, and I am about to leave and take Nikki home for the night, and I think that your photographers are ready to go themselves," Adrian explained, pointing toward the photographer.

"Adrian, with everything going on, I forgot that they were still here! Well, let's go and take a few more pictures together, so that they can leave," Shayla said, looking over at Hubert.

"Baby, I have taken more than enough pictures for one day. Get one more of Nikki, and you guys can take as many as you want. But remember, we have to get out of here in a little bit," Hubert told Adrian, smiling and nodding his head as if he had something up his sleeve for when they leave.

Adrian laughed, and said, "Aw, man, please, you guys have years for that mess. And speaking of that, where is Donovan, anyway?"

They all looked around but Donovan was nowhere to be found right then.

"Well, can you tell him that I am taking some pictures with Shay, and then I am going to take Nikki home? Tell him I will be back in a few minutes, and, Hue, please don't let him drink that much tonight," Adrian pleaded.

Hubert responded softly, "I will try, Adrian, and can you kiss my little girl for me, and tell her that daddy loves her, and will bring her back a souvenir from Hawaii."

Shayla and Adrian took a few more pictures before Adrian left, and Hubert continued to mingle with the guests, when he finally linked back up with Donovan, who was with a face unfamiliar to Hubert. Donovan did not handle his liquor that well, and was not normally a drinker, so Hubert always found that he had to look after him when he drinks.

"Hey, man, look who I found," Donovan said. "He told me that he works with you."

"The wedding was nice, man," he said, holding his hand out for Hubert to shake.

Hubert looked at him strangely, wondering where or if he had ever seen his guy before. "You work with me at J. Marshall Marketing?"

"Yes, sir. Well, I start Monday," he explained. "Clayton Lewis. I should be working right in your department. Hey, I heard that you all had a crazy wild night at the bachelor party," he said, reaching to give Hubert a handshake again. "You are the man, playa!"

Hubert looked at Donovan, covered his mouth with his pointer finger, looked back at Clayton, and asked, "Clayton, is that your name?"

"Yeah, my friends call me C-Nice."

"Well, Clayton, you were not by any chance there last night, were you?"

Clayton said, smiling, "I wish."

"So who told you about it?'

"I am staying with one of your other workers, EP. Eric Patterson, he was there and he told me how off the chain it was."

"E told you this?"

"Yeah, he said that you guys were good friends, and he learns a lot from you. To tell you the truth, I am not even going to lie, that cat worships you. He talks like you were the pimp of the century or something."

Hubert looked around to see whether Shayla was close by as Clayton continued to ramble on.

"That kid told me that I needed to bring a pen and a pad with me because you were the professor of mackology 101, and I could learn a lot from you."

Hubert again looked around, and then looked at Donovan, and then back at Clayton, scratched his head, and start talking quietly. "First lesson, those days are over now, I am a married man," he said, flashing the ring in front of Clayton's face.

Clayton looked at him with a very sneaky look on his face, smiled and reached out his hand again for another handshake, and said, "Yeah, right. I am looking forward to working with you. Enjoy your honeymoon."

Clayton walked off, and Hubert looked over at Donovan with a strange look on his face. "I am going to have to keep an eye on that guy."

"Yeah, you are probably right," said Donovan.

"Hey, where is E anyway?" asked Hubert.

"The last time I seen him, he was dancing with some honey on the floor, so no telling where he is right now," answered Donovan looking around. "There he is, over by the bar."

Donovan and Hubert walked over to the bar toward Eric Patterson, better known as EP, who also worked with Hubert at J. Marshall Marketing. Eric was sitting at the bar having a drink, talking to a young lady he met at the reception. Eric had been working with Hubert for almost two years, and Hubert was his trainer, so the two were good friends. Eric looked up to Hubert, and always came to him for advice; most of the time, it was something to do with a woman. As the two got closer, Eric smiled and stood, ready to hug and congratulate Hubert.

"Congrats, boss, you did it," said Eric, shaking Hubert's hand and giving him a hug.

"Thanks, partner," answered Hubert. "So who is your friend?"

"Oh, yeah. Diane, meet the man who taught me almost everything I know, and keeps me on my toes at work."

Hubert reached out his hand to shake the young lady's. "Hubert. And I am glad to meet you."

"I know who you are, and the pleasure is all mine," Diane said, with her hand still out. "Nice reception. I'm sorry that I did not make the wedding. Shayla and I get our hair done at the same salon, and she invited me."

"Well, I am happy that you made it," responded Hubert.

They were all looking at Donovan, when Eric grabbed Diane's hand and turned it toward Donovan. "And this is Donovan Price, Hubert's best friend. He ain't nobody," Eric explained laughing.

"Hi, Donovan."

"What's up, shorty," Donovan said, nodding his head to Diane.

"So, Hubert, where is the new bride anyway?" asked Diane.

"I don't know, she was taking more pictures, but I hope that she is ready to go." Hubert looked around and spotted Shayla. "There she is over there, still stuffing her little face."

"Well, I am going to go over and speak to her," Diane said, grinning at Hubert's last statement. "It was nice meeting you both, and Eric, do not forget to give me an answer before you leave."

Diane walked over to Shayla, and they hug and begin talking. Meanwhile, Hubert and Donovan were staring at Eric with their hands over their mouths as in disbelief. Hubert reached over and softly popped Eric in the back of his head.

"Man, I have been married for only a couple of hours, and you have taken over already. Pimp!" Hubert added, smiling.

"Man, she told me that she rode with her girlfriends, but she wants me to take her home."

"To your house or her house?" asked Donovan.

"She had too much to drink, and I do not want to take advantage of her," Eric explained.

"Man, I would take that big-eyed broad and…" shouted Donovan.

Just as Donovan was about to speak further, Adrian walked back into the reception, and just in time. Hubert put his hands up as if he were telling Donovan *do not say a word* when he noticed Adrian walking in. "Look," Hubert said as he turned Donovan toward Adrian. "There is your girl. You go over there, and I will handle this."

Donovan walked away, saying softly but loud enough so that Hubert and Eric can hear, "I give good advice too. He always thinks he is the only one that can give good advice, punk. But that broad does have big eyes."

Hubert and Eric laughed as Donovan walked over and gave Adrian a hug, and they both walked over to talk with Shayla and Diane. Hubert wrapped his arm around Eric, and they began to walk in the opposite direction.

"Look, if she has too much to drink, still take her home, wherever she wants to go, but whatever you do, do not sleep with her. Because, one, she may not remember, and, two, she may think that you took advantage of her. So take her home, offer her something to eat or drink, you can even put her in bed and she may just fall off to sleep, or she maybe still feeling horny, but whatever the case, if you think that she is too drunk, do not sleep with her. If things work out right, you will be in her pants tomorrow night, if not in the morning after breakfast. Remember, it is all about respect, and if your game is tight as you claim, you should be able to maintain yourself for one night."

"Yeah, you're right as usual," Eric said as he leaned forward to give Hubert a hug. "Thank you, man. Now you and the wifey had better get ready to leave, so you guys can practice doing the hula before you leave for Hawaii, if you know what I mean?"

"You have a point," Hubert said, nodding his head. "So let me go and get my new bride, so we can say our good byes and leave on up out of here. By the way, shorty does have enormous eyes, but they are beautiful. Handle your business, man," Hubert said, laughing.

Hubert found Shayla, and they both went around, hugging and thanking everyone for coming, and letting everyone know when they would be back from their honeymoon, and then the two left.

3

On-the-Job Training

While Hubert and Shayla were away on their honeymoon, Clayton was trying to fit in. He was trying to learn all that he could about everyone. Now Clayton was very sneaky, and could amaze you with his up-front questioning, along with the smirky look he would have on his face. He always looked as if he either knew something or he was up to something. Being that Hubert was going to be training Clayton and was away, there was really nothing he could do until he returned, so they used him wherever they felt necessary. This really did not matter in the least to Clayton because he got to know more people's business this way. He was asked to deliver an envelope to Alisha Coleman's desk, and instantly he found the conversationalist he had been searching for.

He walked up and knocked at the open door.

Alisha, who was on the phone at the time, waved him in. Alisha was attractive, about five foot six or five foot seven, a hundred thirty pounds, brown-skinned, with long hair that was actually hers. She was also somewhat educated, so immediately Clayton was caught off guard. He walked in and did not say a word, holding the forms behind his back as if he had forgotten why he was there in the first place.

Once she got off the phone, she asked, "Can I help you?"

"Oh! I am supposed to deliver these forms to you," Clayton explained, smiling.

"And you are?"

Pausing and starting the sentence off the same way as the last, Clayton replied, "Oh, I am Clayton, Clayton Lewis," as he held out his hands to shake hers. "I am going to be training with Mr. Alexander upstairs when he gets back from his honeymoon."

"Oh yeah, that fool did do that, didn't he?" Alisha said, shaking her head. "I feel for her."

Clayton boldly responded, "And why is that, shorty? What are you trying to say?"

Not really wanting to comment, Alisha took the envelope from Clayton, and started opening it and taking the papers out. "What did you say your name was again?"

"Clayton, but all of my friends call me C-Nice."

"And why is that?"

"I guess it is because of the way I handle a basketball."

"So I guess you are pretty good, huh?"

"All I can say is that I am nice," Clayton said, laughing, pushing his two hands up in the air as if he were shooting a jump shot.

"Well C-Nice, it is nice meeting you. My name is—well, I guess you know my name is Alisha Coleman"—pointing to her nameplate on the door. She then took out her lipstick from her purse on the desk and began applying it slowly to her lips. "My friends call me Peaches." Pointing to him with the lipstick still in her hand—"And don't ask why!"

"Well, nice to meet you too," Clayton added as he began to walk out.

She stood up to put the envelope in a file cabinet. "Hey, C."

Clayton looked back, speechless and stunned by her entire physical package while she was standing.

She smiled, knowing that he was watching her body, because it was entirely too obvious. "Maybe we can do lunch one day, and I can give you the lowdown on everyone here."

Clayton walked back in, smiling. "Maybe even dinner one night."

"Let us just leave it at lunch for right now. Thanks for the forms."

"It was my pleasure," Clayton added and then walked out.

"I bet," Alisha said to herself quietly.

Clayton walked out, so extremely impressed with Peaches that he was searching for someone to tell. He ran into Eric getting on the elevator.

"You a busy man, aren't you, player? I see you everywhere."

"No, I just had to drop some mail off upstairs. And by the way man, what's the story on that cutie?" Clayton paused, trying to remember her name. "Man, all I know that she is named after a fruit—plum, pear, raisin…"

They both walked out of the elevator, and started walking together down a hall, with Clayton still thinking and Eric laughing.

"Man, I just think that you are just hungry. But I am pretty sure that you are talking about Peaches Coleman."

"Peaches, yeah, that's it. That chick got mad gifts."

"She's hot, but she is a little different. She is Einstein smart but OJ Simpson attitude when she does not get her way. Good girl, I love her to death, but she is kind of on the spoiled side. I think Moms and Pops gave her too much, without enough discipline, and she thinks that the world owes her. And when she does not get things the way she wants them…" Eric shakes his head, looking down. "It is a sad day on the job for anyone that crossed her path."

"Wow."

"Yeah, wow is right."

"She did tell me that she would go out to lunch with me one day and give me the scoop on everyone. What do you think about that?"

Eric looked Clayton up and down a couple times with a very serious look on his face. "Maaan!"

"What?"

"Man, look, don't get caught up in this mess in your first couple of weeks here. You know how jobs are. Just like high school, every group has its cliques. Some people are liked, like the athletes and cheerleaders, and some are not liked, like the nerds, but everyone is talked about for something. Just like reality television, people need conflict or disagreement to make the world go round, so if there is nothing to talk about, they find something, even if they have to make it up. Personally, I love your trainer, Hue, and I have learned a lot from him, because for one, he keeps it real, and he does not care what anyone says about him. Because trust me, they all talk about him. But he does not sling mud back, or start any altercations like some congressional debate. He always told me, if the rumor is true, eat it, but keep it to yourself, regardless what people say. You truly have only one person to answer to, and I do not think he works with you."

"Alexander hit, didn't he? That is why shorty was so negative about him getting married. He probably didn't smack it up, flip it, and rub it down like he was supposed to."

"C-Nice, didn't I tell you that I am not putting anyone's business out like that. Come on, man!"

"E, you make this cat sound like some kind of philosopher, while others are making him sound like a pimp. What's the story, man?"

"I am not going to say that Hue did or does everything right, I am just saying that he makes sense when it comes to dealing with people. And I do not want you to get with Peaches and have an assumption about any people on our team before you give them the benefit of the doubt."

"Man, I am not trying to assume nothing, I am trying to find a way to get in this cutie's pants. So if I have to hear about how trifling your boy Alexander, you, or even the owner of the company is, I am going to listen and go to as many lunches as possible and keep on listening. Look, are you sure that you are not trying to stop me from hitting because you want to hit?"

Eric stopped near an open room and stared at Clayton, who continued to walk. Clayton, then realizing that Eric had stopped, also stopped and looked back. Eric said, "It ain't that type of party, C-Nice. I come here to work, and I am not trying to block any kind of game you are trying to play. I just want you to watch yourself. But that is all right, man, do your thing!"

"E, why you upset with me, man?" Clayton asked, walking toward Eric.

"I'm good, but I do have work to do, so I will holler at you later."

Clayton walked closer to Eric for a handshake-hug kind of deal, but on Eric's face one could tell that he did not care too much for Clayton at that moment. "I do appreciate all the info. I will eat the meat and spit out the bones."

Clayton then walked off, and after Eric walked in the open room he heard Clayton calling his name. "Yo, E?"

Eric walked back and as soon as he got to the door, Clayton leaned his head in the room so fast that he almost head-butted Eric in the face. "You all right, man?" Eric asked, looking at Clayton bewildered.

"Yeah, I'm straight, I was just wondering when my man Alexander was coming back. I thought he would be back by now."

"I guess Monday, as far as I know."

"Man, that is going to be almost two weeks. I wish that I had it like that. What are you doing when you get off, anyway?"

"I don't know yet. Maybe I will get my new roommate to finally put most of his mess away, and put in storage what he doesn't need."

"I got you, man."

Clayton walked back through, and noticed that Hubert's office door was open. As he peeped in, he saw Hubert sitting at his desk, bent over, placing papers in his bottom drawer. Clayton knocked.

"What's up, young man, come on in," Hubert said, looking up.

"You are back early, aren't you?"

"No, I still have today and the weekend, but I had to look at some papers. How have they been treating you around here?"

"It's cool, getting to know a few people, but mostly running errands. I feel like the mail carrier."

"I completely understand, but I guess you have to start somewhere."

"Yo, I know that the honeymoon was nice," Clayton said with his head tilted and smiling, looking out the corner of his eyes.

Hubert stared quietly at him for about five seconds. "Yeah, it was nice."

"You didn't make any babies out there, did you?"

Looking through a filing cabinet, as if he did not want to answer that question because it was way too personal, Hubert replied softly, "Naw, nothing like that."

Still digging for information. "So do you want any kids?"

Hubert, still looking through the filing cabinet, stopped and looked up at Clayton but did not say a word. But in his mind, he was wondering why this guy was asking all of these questions.

Clayton then placed his hand on his mouth with an incredulous look on his face. "Oh snap, that's right, you have a daughter by your boy's girl. Ya'll got some young and the restless type mess going on around this place."

Clayton laughed but Hubert looked at him without a smile on his face, still saying nothing.

"My bad, man. I can't help it, stuff like this is wild. You don't hear stories like this every day. It is like some Jerry Springer *Montel Williams* type situation. It's like—"

"Did you need something, Clayton?" Hubert butted in.

"Naw, man, I was just welcoming you back, and letting you know that I am ready for training whenever you are ready. And being you have gotten married before my training, along with my training can you spit some of that mad player's game down to me that I have been hearing about, so I can get down too?"

Hubert finally pulled an envelope out of the desk and smiled, shaking his head from side to side in disbelief of what he was hearing, but the next statement took it even further.

"I see that you are smiling. What do you have in the envelope, naked pictures or something, because I want to see, can I see?"

Hubert was still shaking his head. He then stood up and looked at Clayton. "You are wild, Clayton."

"Why, man?"

Not wanting to go into it, Hubert just responded, "Clayton, I will see you Monday."

Hubert started gathering all of his things, not even looking up at Clayton, implying that he wanted him to leave, but then sat back down. Clayton stood for about a minute not saying anything, instead watching Hubert's every move as if he were studying him for a project. Hubert began plundering through his things like he was in the room alone, not paying any attention to Clayton.

Clayton, now looking upset, "All right, man, I will see you Monday! You're a trip and your boy makes it seem like you were this all-American first-class and top-of-the-line pimp that everyone likes and listened to."

Clayton stared at Hubert with this upsetting, serious look on his face. At the same time Hubert's expression never changed. He just continued to shake his head, looking down, putting a Bible into a briefcase.

"A Bible!" Clayton yelled out. "All that mess you do, and you have the audacity to carry around a Bible."

Before he could get the word *Bible* out of his mouth good, Hubert stood up with his briefcase in his right hand and pointing at Clayton with his left. "First of all, it's a children's Bible, my daughter goes to church with my mother sometimes, and left it here. Second, you do not know me to judge me. Third, I am who I am because of who I am, and not based on what other people make me out to be. Lastly—no, better yet, man, get out of my office so that I can go home!"

"I am out, man, but you are a trip!" Clayton finally walked out of the door.

"Bye, Clayton."

Hubert grabbed all of his things and walked out of the office. He looked around for cameras before turning off the lights, in his mind thinking, what just happened, and could this be real or was he on some crazy employee reality TV show?

As Hubert was walking through the hall, he noticed Clayton talking to Eric, mouthing off like he was upset about something. Hubert, being a bold individual, walked right over and gave Eric a hug and a pound. "EP, what's up?"

"Nothing. What's up with you newlywed?'

"All is well, all is well."

"You are back early, aren't you?"

"Can a man not come to the job and pick up a few things from his office while on vacation?"

At that point, Clayton looked over at Eric making a face expressing *Do you see what I mean?*

Eric immediately brushed him off and went on with the conversation. "So are you going to teach this man how to run the marketing business?" Pointing at Clayton.

"This man don't seem to keep his mouth closed long enough to even learn how to run a lawn mower." Hubert smiled and looked over at Clayton for his facial reaction.

Clayton, who seemed to always want to talk about everyone one else, seemed offended by the comment and did not find it the least bit funny. Eric, on the other hand, covered his mouth like he wanted to laugh. But when he realized the tension between the two, he looked at the both of them, smiled at Hubert, and looked back at Clayton. "Come on, C, you have been on the prowl continuously for you only being here a week and some change, trying to hunt down all the information that you can about everybody."

"I figured you would agree with him," Clayton replied angrily shaking his head.

"Naw, C, I can't help it. You act like you work for CNN."

"Man, look, are you going to give me a ride home or do you want me to walk?"

Laughing before he even answered the question, Eric responded, "I don't know why you are trying to look all hard anyway when you need a ride home. I would tell you to walk home"—looking down at Clayton's shoes—"but with those busted kicks you don't need to walk home, you need to walk to the mall."

Hubert was trying not to laugh, but could not help it, although he did avoid looking down at the shoes.

With an angry and embarrassed look on his face, "Man, I'll find my own way home!"

And Clayton turned and walked off.

"Aw, the little tall man is mad," Eric taunted Clayton as if he were a child. "Give me fifteen minutes, man, and I will be out."

Clayton walked off not saying a word, feeling embarrassed, and before he could turn and be out of their sight, Eric yelled out, "C-Nice."

"What?"

"I do like your shoes. I think that they are cute."

Clayton threw up his middle finger and walked out of the building and out of sight.

Eric and Hubert burst out in laughter.

"Your boy is wild," Hubert said, looking at Eric.

"Yeah, he is a little different."

"I don't think he is going to like me, but really I do not care."

Eric tried to defend him. "He is cool most of the time. He is just one of those jealous brothers that hate on other brothers that may be doing better than him. He is just doing his thing, being the All-American Hater. By the way, he is a State alum just like you and your boy Donovan."

"I am going to have to keep an eye on him."

"Everyone had better. And another thing, he is mad nosey, so remember that when you are training him."

"I got him, just watch your back. All right, I have to get back to the wife."

Eric leaned forward, and gave Hubert a hug and pound. "It sounds funny hearing you say that of all people."

"It sounds funny to me sometimes too, but it's all good so far, and I have a good girl. Spoiled, but good."

"Yeah, you're right. So, have you been by DA-Station's yet?

"No, not yet, but if I am able to sneak out for a few minutes tonight, I will give you a call. Monday we will start the round table back up."

"All right, I am out. Congratulations again."

Eric and Hubert left walking separate ways.

DA-Station was Donovan's restaurant/night club. It was an old train station that had not been used for years. After Donovan graduated from college, his dream was to open his own club, and he used his management degree and people skills to take it to the next level. However his credit was not good enough to obtain a loan so he did not have the money to make this dream a reality. This is how Adrian came into the picture. Her father had unfortunately passed away after a short fight with cancer. He was diagnosed in June and died in August. Before he had gotten sick, he purchased a healthy life insurance plan to avoid running into the same problem he had with his wife, Adrian's mother, who was killed in a car accident when Adrian was only ten. Adrian's father, then in the military, did not have life insurance on his wife, and in turn they struggled with funeral arrangements, her left-behind bills, and childcare for Adrian when he was on deployments. He did not want to leave Adrian in a similar bind as he had been in. So after her father passed away, Adrian was left with a substantial amount of money to take care of all of his business and still have money to live.

Adrian eventually met Donovan through Hubert, and they hit it off and she decided she would help him finance his dream. She fronted the money and credit, and became the co-owner of the restaurant—the *D* and *A* of DA-Station stood for Donovan and Adrian. The couple's relationship was just as successful as the restaurant. Donovan wanted to get married, but she liked things the way they were right then. Even though they lived together and things were going great, part of her reason for resistance to the nuptials was the fact that she thought that deep down it bothered Donovan that she had a daughter by Hubert and that they had an excellent relationship from childhood. Donovan and Adrian's business and personal relationship was so great on the surface you would think they had been married for years.

DA-Station was the hangout-after-work spot for many of the locals in the area. It was a nice setup with a nice atmosphere. There was a bar with several big screens to watch sports, and anything you'd want to drink while enjoying the television. There was an excellent menu with everything from grilled cheese and soup to lobster and shrimp. There was also a room with pool tables, old video games, dartboards, and they would have an occasional spades tournament that Donavan and Hubert were the reigning champs at. On Wednesday through Saturday, the games room was more like a club environment, with music playing, dancing, and a lot of drinking. The club would stay open until two thirty on these nights, but all other nights, it would shut down at twelve. DA's was a very nice spot for just hanging out.

The "Round Table" was where some of the guys would meet after work, and, before drinking too much, would have a brief discussion on any topic where everyone at the round table (which is actually square) could weigh in. Their topics would range from sports, women, and politics, to religion, children, or what happened at work that day. The others would just follow whoever had the most interesting topic.

Later that evening, Eric and Clayton arrived at the restaurant early to put something in their stomachs before they started drinking, because it was Friday, and they knew that it would probably be a late night. Eric walked in first.

"Good evening, sir, how many are in your party?" asked the hostess.

"Thanks, but we're good, we are going to the bar," Eric replied as he saw Donovan behind the bar with a towel on his shoulder.

Donovan noticed him, smiled, and came from behind the counter to meet them. "EP. What's up, young man?" The two hug and pound.

"I can't call it, bro. What's up with you? I see you back behind the bar. What, you can't find good help, or are you drinking on the job?"

"No, my bartender stepped away for a minute, and I was just covering." The two laughed while Clayton looked around the restaurant in amazement.

"You remember my new roommate, Clayton, right? He was the point guard at State, yours and Hue's old alma mater. They call him C-Nice."

Donovan reached out to shake Clayton's hand. "What's up yo, I think I met you at the reception?"

Clayton was still in awe about the restaurant; even as he reached out his hand to shake Donovan's, he still looked around. "This whole place is yours?"

"Yeah, my girl and I own it together."

"Man, this joint is all that!"

"Thank you, my man. I think I remember you playing now. Didn't you blow out your knee at the beginning of last year?"

"Yeah, unfortunately that was me. My knee has not been the same since. So they let me keep the scholarship and I did graduate in June."

"Good for you, man. So you guys eating or just drinking?"

Eric leaned back and rubbed his stomach. "I am hungry as three people, and if I start drinking now, you will see it again in about an hour and a half." Eric, who was not a seasoned drinker, would often drink without eating, which would eventually lead him to a bathroom, crouched over a toilet vomiting. So he knew that he had to eat first. "Get me that shrimp and fry platter."

Donovan laughed. "No, I am going to point you to the seats at the bar, and the bartender is going to get you whatever you want. Enjoy your meal, gentlemen. And E, make sure you get me your receipt, your money is still no good here."

"What about me?" Clayton asked.

"I don't know you like that, player," Donovan said, looking at Eric.

"What kind of mess is this? You sound just like one of Alexander's boys!"

"Actually, I was just kidding, but Eric helped me to put this place together, so I do owe him. But you are good for tonight. And what's with the Alexander comment anyway, isn't he out of town?"

Clayton again seeming to be speaking out of turn, "No he made his grand entrance to his office this evening." Clayton looked at Eric, waiting for him to say something in some form of defense for Hubert.

Eric just looked at Clayton and shook his head, then looked back at Donovan. Donovan, now lost in the conversation, grabbed his towel and made an expression like he had nothing to do with it, and again pointed to the bar. "Like I said, the bartender is going to get you whatever you want." He then walked off.

So Clayton and Eric enjoyed a meal at DA's, while at the same time Hubert was at home with his new wife, figuring out how he is going to get out for the night.

"Baby, what are you doing?" Hubert asked Shayla.

"I am so tired, but I'm still trying to unpack some of this mess, being that my new husband decided he wanted to dip on me this morning and not help."

Hubert walked up behind her and placed his hands tightly around her waist, and kissed her on the cheeks. "You say 'new husband' like you had an old one. Is there something that you are not telling me?"

Shayla elbows him in the stomach, and responded, smiling, "Yeah, my old husband did not just get home and think that he immediately had to return to work and stay away for hours. My old husband would have helped me unpack, and probably would have fixed me breakfast in bed this morning after last night."

Hubert again came up behind Shayla, wrapping his arms around her waist, and softly whispered, in her ear, as if he were going to say something romantic, "Wow, maybe I should have married him."

Again he got elbowed in the stomach as Shayla looked at him without even the smallest existence of a smile on her face. "Don't play with me, Hue. Hand me that bag over there with all of your souvenirs in it"—pointing to the bag.

"What are you going to do with them?" Hubert asked.

"I am going to put them away."

"Put them away where?" Hubert asked holding on to the bag.

"In the closet, I guess."

"No, don't put them in there. A lot of those souvenirs are for my family and friends." Just then, it hit him how he could get out of the house and hang at DA's with Donovan. "I have a sweater for my mom, a stuffed animal for Nikki, and some key rings and shot glasses for Donovan and Adrian. As a matter of fact, I think I may run over to my mom's and Donovan's spot and drop them off now, while you are still unpacking, unless you want to ride with me"—hoping she would say no—"You are almost finished anyway, right?"

"Hue, you left some time this morning, and now you expect me to keep on unpacking while you go out again?"

"You don't have much left."

"That's not the point."

"So what is the point, baby?" Hubert asked in a sarcastic manner.

"Baby, nothing! You did not marry a maid, and you are not going to be just leaving me here all the time, gallivanting with your friends and mess!"

"Shay, you act like I am asking you to go hang out at the club or something. All I wanted to do is run by my mom's, and Donovan's, and drop off some souvenirs. That is all, baby, wow! I asked if you wanted to ride with me."

As Hubert finished with a guilt-trip attempt, Shayla looked at him, shaking her head and answered, "No, Hue, go right ahead, just be home before it gets dark. Because you and I both know that you can't stop by Donovan's without having a drink or two, but don't get stupid knowing that you have to drive on that road."

"Okay," Hubert answered with a smile on his face, thinking to himself that he did not think it would be this easy to get out. "Are you sure that you don't want to ride?"

"No, Hue, just remember what I told you."

Hubert went through the bag, picking out the souvenirs he planned to take with him, and went downstairs where he placed them in a plastic bag. He then returned upstairs, kissed Shayla, and left.

On his way, he called his mother on the phone. "Hello, Mother."

"God bless you, son," she responded. "I see you and your new bride made it back home safe."

"Yeah, we got in the other night, and the trip was off the chains."

"Off the what?"

"The trip was very nice, Mom. Look, I picked you up some souvenirs, but I am going to have to bring them to you tomorrow, all right?"

"Okay, just call me before you come, to make sure I am here. We have a church meeting tomorrow at one, and I do not know how long it is going to last."

"Okay, Mom, I will do that. I will talk to you later.

"So are you guys coming to church Sunday?"

Hubert riding down the road talking to himself with the phone away from his mouth, "I knew that that was coming."

"Pastor is preaching on a good series right now. You and Shayla need to come on in and receive some. Being you guys are newly married and all. Boy, you need to understand that the devil does not want to see anyone happy, and his plan is to seek and destroy, and our only real defense is a true relationship with God, and then it is still tough a lot of the time. So you guys come on out on Sunday, and let God bless you real good. After that, come on over to the house and let me fix you something to put some meat on both of you guys' bones. Speaking of bones, how is my grandbaby doing?"

With a sigh of relief Hubert answered, "Nikki is doing great, Mom. As a matter of fact, I am going to call her right now, so can I talk to you tomorrow?"

"So will I see you Sunday?"

"I will call you, Mom, talk to you later."

"God be with you, son."

With no real intentions of calling his daughter, Hubert finished his phone conversation with his mom, right when he was pulling up to DA–Station's. He took the sweater out of his bag that he bought for his mother, and took the rest of the items into the restaurant. As he walked in, he saw that Clayton and Eric were still sitting at the bar, so he walked on over.

"I see you made it back out," said Eric.

"Yeah, I am not going to be out long, just going to drop off some souvenirs for my man," Hubert explained.

"What did you bring me?" Clayton asked with his voice slightly slurred from the alcohol.

"Aw, E, you don't let this man drink. I know that I got to go now."

"Naw, man, don't leave, have one drink with me, I'll buy," Eric said holding his hand up to get the bartender's attention. When the bartender looked over, Eric yelled out, "Two rum and Cokes, and"—looking at Hubert—"a double shot of Tanqueray and tonic, with a twist of lime. See, Hue, I remember, right?"

Hubert nodded his head in agreement, and Eric reached over and gave Hubert a high five.

Clayton, who was now a little intoxicated and still seeming a little envious of either Hubert or the relationship between Hubert and Eric, shook his head in disbelief. "Aw, Lord, here we go again. I surely hope that I have somebody to ride my jock one day like this fool rides yours."

Appearing a little frustrated, Hubert looked over at Clayton and slowly rubbed his hand down his face, stopping when only his mouth and chin were covered. He examined Clayton just as if he were interviewing him. "Man, what is your problem?"

Just then Donovan walked over and took a seat beside Clayton, noticed the tension, and immediately wanted to relax the hostility. "The next round is on the house, but that is going to be enough for you fellows for today." Looking at Clayton and Eric. "What's in the bag, pimp?" Donovan asked Hubert. Hubert got up and gave Donovan a handshake and hug.

"Oh, I brought back some souvenirs for you and the girls. The shot glass is for you, and key rings are for Adrian, and the hula bear is for my baby," Hubert explained.

"Thanks," Donovan responded as he took the bag from Hubert. "So, how long are you out, and have you eaten yet?"

"No, I have not eaten yet," Hubert answered, smiling, "and I am going to leave right after I finish that drink you promised on the house. Shay told me not to drink, but you know that I need a little taste to get me through, then I guess I will go home and eat with the wife, like I am supposed to do. What do you think?"

"That married life is for you now, buddy. I need to work on my foundation a little more. I would hate to lose half, but I want to get married too. So I will be keeping a close eye on you," Donovan said, laughing.

Intoxicated and thinking he was speaking in a soft whisper, Clayton leaned over and told Eric, "From what I heard, she owns over half already."

Eric, the peacemaker, knowing that everyone heard the comment, including Donovan, elbowed Clayton in the ribs. Clayton looked at him knowing that he may have said something wrong, because the only way he would have known this information was if Eric had told him, in turn placing Eric on the spot too. The table was completely silent for a few seconds, like they were observing a moment of silence or something, then Eric spoke out, shaking his head.

"You act stupid when you drink, man. I am not going anywhere else with you!"

Now embarrassed, Clayton retaliated with, "No, man, you stupid."

Eric, now upset for many reasons, finished his drink and stood up. "Sorry, fellas, let me carry this drunk home."

"Are you all right on the road?" asked Hubert.

"I'm good, I only had a few, because I was planning on coming back out tonight. But if I do, I can promise you it will be alone, and not with Ned the Wino." Clayton started staggering to the door and then looked back to see if Eric was following him, but Eric was still talking. "You coming back out tonight?"

"Not tonight, playa, the wife got me tonight, and I promised to be back before it gets dark. I am new in this thing so I want to start doing right for a few minutes, and the marriage just may last for years. But you take your boy home."

"You really need to reevaluate your friends you move in your house. Your boy is trouble and I would hate to ban him from my club, but either I am going to do that, or I am going in his mouth the next time he disrespects me. And I am as serious as I look," Donovan said with an extremely serious look on his face.

"My bad, guys, I have never seen him drink like this," Eric tried to explain.

Hubert added, "E, his problem is more than drinking. He has to—"

But just as Hubert was about to finish his sentence, Clayton yelled out, "Come on, man!"

Donovan reached out and gave Eric a quick hug and pound, but immediately told him, "Get that boy out of my club right now!"

"I got you. Sorry, fellas, I really am," Eric said as he walked to the door, grabbing Clayton by the arm to help hold him up, and they both walked out the door.

"I know that E is mad. He thought that he was going to get his swerve on tonight when the ladies started coming in. I guess I had better be getting out here too, after I finish this drink. I will call tomorrow, and probably come by the house and see my baby."

"Word. Take your time on the drink, I am going back here to check on the setup for later." The two shook hands, and Hubert finished his drink, and Donovan headed for the back.

Hubert finished his drink, jumped in his truck and headed back home to his wife, remembering she said to be home before dark, so he knew that he was in the clear this time. He walked in the house smiling, not noticing the lights were out, and candles were lit, because his focus was on knowing he had beaten his curfew. Shayla immediately approached him in some sexy lingerie that would make the average man's mouth drop. He just stared at her, speechless.

She walked up to him, hugged him, and whispered softly in his ear, "I waited for you with dinner. I love you, but I am going to bed. Dinner is on the table, and could you please blow out the candles when you're done?" She kissed him on the cheeks, and began walking upstairs. She was upset, but handling it so well. As she reached the top of the stairs, she yelled down, "So how is your mom doing?"

Hubert just looked up in a confused state as she walked into the bedroom, still thinking in his mind, *I am on time.* As he walked into the kitchen, he saw one side of the perfect candlelit dinner. He looked up, thinking maybe he needed to go and talk to his wife, then he looked at dinner. He looked back up, and then back at dinner again, and decided to go ahead and sit down and eat, being it was there and he was hungry. After dinner, when it seemed like the perfect opportunity to go upstairs and talk, he then decided to fix him a drink before he went up. Finally, he finished the drink, blew the candles out, and he made his way to the bedroom. Shayla was lying in bed with her back turned to him, not asleep, but Hubert could not tell. He walked in and sat on the other side of the bed and started talking off his shoes.

"Baby," he called.

"Yes, Hue?"

"Are you mad at me?"

"No, Hue."

"What's wrong, because if you are not mad you are *something* with me," Hubert had the audacity to ask in a sarcastic manner.

"Go to sleep, Hue."

Hubert then, in a playful manner, leaned over and placed his mouth right on her ear, and said, "I'm sorry, I suck."

"You smell like gin. Are you drunk?"

"No, I just fixed me a drink before I came up here."

Shayla turned toward him, and sat up on the bed. "You mean that you think that I am mad at you, and you actually ate and fixed a drink, before you came up! Look, baby, I know that we had a great time in Hawaii, and I know that you have to get back to reality, but one, you seemed to be more anxious to get back to work and to your friends, and two, Hubert Alexander, I think you lied to me about going over your mother's house just to give you more time at the club."

"I—"

Shayla put her hands over his lips before he could start talking. "Don't say anything, I am not finished. My mother said that obtaining a marriage was very easy, it's the maintaining that is the hard part. I want to stay on the honeymoon forever, but honesty would be a great characteristic for us to start with, you think?"

"Wow," Hubert uttered as he gathered his thoughts. "I am sorry, I was going to go over my mother's, but I did think that it would cut into my time at DA's."

"But—"

"No, let me talk. I understand exactly where you are coming from, and I was wrong, and I am sorry." He leaned over and pecked her softly on the lips, and then came along with a longer, passionate kiss, but during the kiss, she moaned for him to stop, pushing him away.

Smiling, she said, with one hand on his chest holding him off, "Man, I have not even accepted your apology yet, what do you think you doing?"

Hubert stood up, walked to her side of the bed, and slowly took his shirt off and unbuckled his pants while smooth-talking at the same time. "Baby, I messed up, dinner was great, and you look extremely sexy tonight." He then began licking his lips, looking at her.

She reached out and grabbed his belt buckle, and looked at him with an innocent smile, shared those words he was hoping for: "You're forgiven." And the rest of that night was history.

4

Hubert Is Propositioned

Hubert was back at work, months have gone by, the honeymoon was over, and it was business as usual.

"Mr. Alexander, you have a phone call."

Hubert hurried to his desk, expecting his call from his boss, who called to make sure that everything was still running smoothly.

"This is Hubert Alexander speaking," he answered.

"Hubert."

"Hi, boss, how are you?"

"I have been better. How are things out there?" he questioned.

Hubert went into some of the daily details of what was going on with the job, and then he paused and asked, "You said that you have been better. Is something wrong, sir?"

"Well, my wife wants me to go out of town with her, and I really do not feel like going."

"Where out of town?"

"Detroit."

"Detroit! What's in Detroit other than Motown and the Pistons, if you do not mind me asking?"

"My stepson lives out there, and I guess he and his wife are having problems. She wants to leave, and he wants her to stay, but she feels that they need some time apart, and he thinks that they just need counseling, and to make a long story short, my wife thinks that we need to butt our noses in, as if they are not confused enough as it is. Speaking of their marriage, how are you and the beautiful new bride doing?"

"Just fine, sir, thanks for asking."

"Hubert, I have known you for many a year, and I remember a lot of the things you have gotten yourself into, and even some things I have gotten you out of. A word of wisdom for you, son: be careful out there. My father used to tell me, when you first get married is when you are the most attractive. And, I Tue, you have been running after skirts for years, so I hope that you know and understand what you have to do. I also hope that you understand that you have made some substantial decisions, when you said *I do*."

"I understand, Dad," Hubert answered laughing.

"I hope that you do. On that note, how is Alisha doing?"

"She is fine, sir, still crazy."

"Well, you made her that way. You know, I do not think I seen her at your wedding?"

"No, sir, she said that you had her doing some special project or something."

"Oh, I do not remember. So did she get you anything?"

"Yeah, an iron to go with the other four that we got."

"By the way, this Clayton Lewis that is working for you—how is he making out? I thought he would be a good fit for you, being you guys went to the same college and played sports."

"Mr. Lewis—or as he likes to be called by his friends, C-Nice—is a mess." Hubert paused for a minute, and then went on, "It is something about him, boss. I don't know if he speaks too freely, is too nosey, or just doesn't care, but I just get bad vibes about this kid. But I could be wrong."

"Just work with him, and see how he does. We will make a decision after a short probationary period."

"Not a problem. Anything for the man that signs my check."

"Hue, I have to get ready to go. Do me a favor and hire one more person to work with Alisha, to ease her workload, and I will be calling you in a week or two. Take it easy, and remember, take heed to what I told you."

"Have a safe flight, Dad. I will be just fine."

Hubert hung the phone up, and then called his wife. He spun around in the chair, facing the back of his office, waiting for Shayla to pick up on the other end.

Meanwhile, Alisha walked in unannounced, and just stood there wondering why he was facing the back of his office.

"Hello, Mrs. Alexander," Hubert said smoothly and softly on the phone. "That sounds nice, don't it, Mrs. Alexander?

How are you feeling? Yeah, I am just fine, I miss my baby. What are your plans for the evening? What do I have in mind? How about I pick up a bottle of Moët, two New York Strips, a few potatoes ready to be baked, and a salad, and we sat by the fire and listen to the smooth jazz sounds of the late, great George Howard. Sounds good? Whatever happens next, I will leave to you. No, I am serious. Look for me around six. I love you too. Bye, baby." Hubert smiled, turned the chair around, and there stood Alisha.

"Aw, that is so cute. A bottle of Moët, a steak, salad, and potato, and we sat by the fire and listen to the smooth jazz sounds of the late great George Howard," Alisha said in a mocking voice. "Did Mr. Marshall say anything about getting me a helper, and do you have my orange Tic Tacs?"

"Yes, he did, and I will get you someone as soon as I can. And here"—Hubert reached in his desk and pulled out a box of orange Tic Tacs, for this was their routine: whenever he purchased peppermint Tic Tacs, he would get her orange.

"Thanks, and, Hubert, can I ask you a question?"

Hubert looked up at Alisha, wondering if the question was job related or personal, because of the look on her face, but he nodded his head.

She began slowly. "Why have you never talked to me like that? I have seen you with other girls, and you are always so sweet, and polite, and a gentleman. What is it with me?"

"Peaches"—Hubert trying to find the right words—"We have a work relationship, and even though I think you are a dime, and everyone thinks we have already done this or that, I have a great deal of respect for you." Hubert's explanation seemed sincere, until he added, "Besides, if I got into your mind, and eventually into your bed, you would be in my office too much, bringing me lunch, cleaning the floor, doing my toenails…"

Alisha immediately interrupted him, putting her hand up for him to stop talking. As she walked out she shook her head.

Later that day while Alisha was in her office, Hubert called on the phone. "Hey, baby, what are you doing?"

"What do you want, Mr. Alexander?"

"I thought about what you said, about how I speak to you, and how I treat you."

"And," Alisha said in a loud voice.

Hubert went on. "Maybe I need to be a little different with you. We have known each other for years, and we both know that the attraction is there."

Alisha, smiling to herself on the other end, wondering where this conversation was going, asked, "Hue, what are you doing?"

"No, I thought maybe one evening after we get off, we could plan to meet somewhere, and"—laughing to himself as he talked—"get a couple of Colt 45s, two Big Macs and some fries, and listen to the late, great Biggie Smalls."

Hubert, trying to sound smooth, burst out in laughter. But added, still laughing, "What do you think?"

"Go to hell, Hue, I still hate you," as she hung up the phone. She did, however, smile, because she did think that it was kind of funny, and as usual she shook her head and went back to work.

Later that week, Alisha was one of the first to arrive on the job, went into her office, and started going through a pile of paperwork, when this slender twenty-something-looking brunette walked in, and tapped on the open door.

"Can I help you?" Alisha asked, wondering why someone was in her office so early in the morning.

"Hi, my name is Christina Douglass, and I heard from a great source that you were hiring. I was told to speak with a Hubert Alexander."

At the first glance, Alisha just stared. Christina was about five foot seven, slim, with a look as if she were born in a gym, very attractive, and standing in a navy-blue tight-fit skirt suit. She looked like wherever she went, even if it were the White House, the job was hers. Just like a woman, this caught Alisha off guard from the start, being a successful, attractive black woman already, so she paused for the first few seconds.

Alisha walked over to Christina from behind her desk. "Hi, I am Alisha Coleman, and if you are hired, you would be working for me."

Now one thing about Alisha: she always dressed to impress, and this was the first thing that Christina noticed. Christina shrugged her shoulders as if to say she did not care who she worked for, but she did let her know right from the start. "Girl, you are wearing that outfit. Where did you get that?"

"I think Anne Klein, or Donna Karen," Alisha answered, smiling because she seemed to be just as impressed with her outfit as Christina was with hers, but she would not let on to it.

"So where are you from, and what do you do?"

"I am from Michigan, and right now, I am willing to do whatever you need me to do to get my foot in the door," Christina explained with a lot of enthusiasm.

"Well, I do need help, but you are going to have to wait and talk to Mr. Alexander, who oversees human resources. He should be in in about an hour."

"Do you think that I stand a chance at getting the job?"

"Christina—or Tina, do you mind if I call you Tina?"

"I would prefer Chris."

"Well, Chris—and you can call me Peaches—if you flaunt your little self around him all positive like you do around me, you will be just fine. And between you and I, that skirt is not going to hurt any either. Don't worry about Alexander. He is a man's man that likes pretty things around him, so if you interview well and have a nice enough resume, I will be training you in a few days."

"Thank you. What time should I expect him?"

"It is about eight fifteen now, so expect him around eight forty-five."

"So where should I wait?"

"There is a lounge around the corner, and when I see him, I will send him to you."

"Thanks, Peaches." "Remember what I said, girl," Peaches added, pointing to the skirt.

Christina gave Peaches a wink and a thumbs-up. She then walked toward the lounge, and Peaches went back to work.

A few minutes later, Peaches was working at her desk when Hubert leaned in and tapped on the door.

"Good morning, precious, how are we?" he asked, smiling.

"I am good," she answered. "Someone seems like they had a good night or something like that."

"I will go with 'something like that.' Besides, I am always in a good mood."

"Don't remind me," Peaches added softly but still so that Hubert could hear, and at the same time rolling her eyes, still thinking about the last phone conversation from days before.

"How was your night?"

"Why?" She then crossed her arm, rolled her neck, and told Hubert in a loud voice, "I went home, and got my Big Mac, and a Colt 45, and fell asleep."

Hubert then remembered what he had told her days earlier, and busted out laughing, pointing at Peaches. "Good one, I forgot about that."

"I bet you did," speaking ironically.

"It was pretty good, if I say so myself. I thought—"

"Look," Peaches said, interrupting him. "You have an interview in the lounge."

"Seriously?" Hubert asked, not expecting anyone. "Have you seen them? Is it a man or a woman?"

"Look"—with her hand up—"her name is Christina Douglass, she is a young, pretty little thing, and she is looking for a job! Could you please go interview her, and leave me alone? I am busy enough as it is. And if you can stop procrastinating on hiring potential candidates, I can get some help around here."

"I got you."

Hubert walked off toward his office, not knowing what to expect from his candidate awaiting him. He went into his office and picked up some interview forms, and then headed for the lounge.

Christina was in the lounge waiting patiently, sitting back in the corner, with her legs crossed, drinking a diet soda, reading a magazine, also not knowing what to expect. In her mind, she was thinking about Peaches's advice about her interviewer, and she looked down at her skirt, and smiled to herself. Just then, Hubert walked in.

"Mrs. Douglass?"

Christina slowly got up out of her seat, placed the magazine back in the magazine rack, and with both hands pulled her closely fitted skirt down. After that, her right hand moved the hair out of her face. Hubert was taken by her beauty so much that through his eyes, he saw her moving in slow motion, and for a split second he went speechless.

She walked over to him with her hand out for a handshake, staring into his eyes, seemingly as intrigued as he was.

"That is *Ms.* Douglass, but Christina or Chris would be just fine," Christina said as she shook Hubert's hand.

"Well, Chris, I am Hubert Alexander. My friends call me Hue, and I will be conducting your interview this morning, so please, if you would follow me to a conference room."

Before they started walking off, they both still stared at each other for a few seconds. This could have been part of Hubert's mack game, but he seemed a little different this time. He then escorted her to the conference room, which was right down the hall. As they walked into the room, Hubert pulled a chair back for her to sit in, and proceeded to walk to the other side of the table.

"Please have a seat, and before we begin, do you have any questions, comments, or concerns?" Hubert asked.

With a giant smile on her face, she answered, "No."

"Can I get you anything to make you feel a little more comfortable? If not, I will go ahead and start."

"I am just fine, Mr. Alexander. You can go ahead and start."

They both seemed a little nervous, which was very uncharacteristic for Hubert, but he knew that he would have to relax, be himself, and break the ice.

"Didn't I tell you to call me Hue?"

Smartly, Christina replied, "No, you said that your friends call you Hue."

"Impressive early in the morning, I see. I hope that your resume is just as impressive." Hubert looked into her eyes with finger resting on his face in a smooth charismatic manner. "But I also hope that we can eventually be friends."

Adjusting her blouse, noticing that Hubert's eyes had made it near her cleavage a couple of times, she responded, still smiling, "That is very possible."

"So can I call you Tina?"

Christina quickly answered, "Not if you expect me to respond to you." They both burst out laughing as if they had known each other for years, and could talk like that. Christina covered her mouth as she laughed because she was laughing so hard, because she could not believe that she had said what she had said in an interview. Hubert stopped laughing and just stared at her, as she continued to be amused by the situation. After about a minute, she got herself together. "I am sorry, I am sorry. No, just Chris, thank you."

"Wow! You are quick on the draw." Hubert began to look over the resume, and the interview actually began to start. "So where are you from?"

"Michigan."

"So what brings you to Virginia?"

"I needed a change."

"Is it working for you so far?"

"I don't know, is it?" with a very flirtatious smile on her face.

Speechless, Hubert continued to look through the resume with the resume up in front of his face so that he did not have Christina in his sight. But every once in a while, he would peep around the paper, and she would catch him each time, and he would just shake his head.

"Sixty-five words per minute, knowledge and experience of all the new software, even software I have never heard of. Steady work histories, seem very dependable, and possibly overqualified. So how did you learn about this job?"

"From a very reliable source," she answered, shaking her head.

"Why do you want this job, and what can you, Christina Douglass, bring to this company?"

"I want the job because I like helping people, and what can I bring to this company? Well, I am honest, hardworking, ready and willing to learn anything to help the company move forward. And why are you looking at me like that?"

"I don't know, but there is something about you that is so relaxing to me. But you can keep talking."

Christina smiled, and pointed at Hubert. "Do you tell this to all the girls you interview? Because you seem like such a flirt."

"No, I am serious. Your personality and confidence level are top of the line, not to mention that—ah. Well, I will keep that to myself. And no, I do not tell that to all of the girls that I interview, and are you married?" Looking down at her ringless ring finger.

Looking lost for a minute, or at least acting lost, she covered her face with both hands and then with her eyes wide open looked at Hubert. "Where did that come from, and what does it have to do with me getting a job, Mr. Alexander?"

Hubert did not feel confused, but he wanted to make sure that everything he was doing or saying was still within company guidelines. "For the next-of-kin purposes, of course. We would not want something to happen to you while you were working for us and we did not know who to get in contact with."

"That is very understandable, and if I am hired, I will give you my momma's number back in Michigan. And if something so happens to me, you can contact her. But I did notice that you were married." Watching his ring finger and having a look on her face like *What do you have to say about that?*

"New gold shines. I just got married a few months ago," Hubert responded as he slowly placed the hand with the wedding ring in his lap.

"Don't hide it now, it must be nice," with the smile quickly removed from her face.

"You are a mess!"

"Do I have the job, Mr. Alexander?" Christina asked as she stood up.

Hubert noticed her change in attitude, and he knew that he was going to have to play this smooth, because he really needed the help, and he was wondering, had he led her on, or was it just good chemistry? He looked at the resume, and then looked at Christina, and the again at the resume, and back at Christina. This time he watched Christina's thighs as she was standing. She immediately noticed this, and with both hands pulled her skirt down, smiling, shaking her head. Hubert smiled back, and then leaned back in his chair.

"When can you start?"

"I can start tomorrow!" Christina said excitedly.

"Well, let us let you get settled in Virginia for a weekend, and come back Monday. On Monday, at nine a.m., you are to meet with Alisha Coleman, who will be your reporting manager. I take it you have already had the pleasure of meeting her?"

"Yes, she is cute."

"Whatever, man, just make sure you have identification and momma's contact number from Michigan." Hubert stood up, came around his desk, and shook Christina's hand. "Welcome to J. Marshall Marketing."

They both stood looking into each other's eyes, smiling for entirely too long. Christina finally pulled her hand back, and walked toward the door real slow, showing her curves as if she were purposely trying to tease Hubert, not knowing that he was not paying attention at the time. When he looked up, he was caught off guard by the way she was walking. He could not help it, and said softly, "Good God!"

Hearing him and knowing exactly what he said, she turned and asked with an innocent look on her face, "Sir, did you say something?"

"No, just good luck, and welcome to the team. Have a safe weekend."

"And Hue," she said in an almost alluring voice, that it caught Hubert off guard.

"Yes?"

"I was married." She smiled, but did not elaborate any more on the issue. She just took her right hand and waved slowly with her fingers. "I hope to see you Monday."

At home, Hubert and Shayla seemed to be having a great marriage, he was home early from work all week, fixing dinner, having fun, and being the best husband he could be, not knowing what lies ahead in the weeks to come.

It was Monday morning, and it was time for work. Shayla, who was a guidance counselor at the high school, left earlier than Hubert. This was good for Hubert, because he took his precious time this morning wanting to impress the new employee. Hubert took pride in being a sharply dressed man, always living by the motto of looking the part. This morning, there was the long, fresh shower with scented gel, the precision shave job, the six-minute teeth brushing and flossing, he even rubbed cucumber under the eyes to eliminate the possible bags. Hubert wanted to look good.

That morning he walked into his office smiling, looking like he was going to an interview, and who would be the first person he runs into but Clayton Lewis.

"What you doing, man, modeling for GQ today?"

"Good morning, Clayton, what do you need?"

"Well, first, I need you to help me in writing this requisition, and second, I wanted to apologize for the way I acted at your boy's club a while back."

"Not a problem, we all have had a little too much to drink from time to time, so it's cool. And you have been doing a good job here," Hubert responded, reaching his hand out for the paper. "It should be line by line, but remember the company's purchase order numbers are in the computers under PON1, a typo we said we would correct when we started the spreadsheet, but all of the information should be in the computer, and we just need this hard copy for our files, so once you input all the information in the computer, you can actually print the requisition, and not write anything, just e-mail me the confirmation number when you get it."

Just then, there was a knock at the door.

"It's open," Hubert yelled out while sitting on his desk.

In walked Alisha and her new trainee, Christina. The expression on Clayton's face immediately changed. He could only stare. The question was, was he staring at Christina or Alisha? But his next sentence made it blatantly obvious.

"Baby, I do not remember your name," as he walked and took Alisha's hand. "So all I am going to say is good morning, Fruity, because I know that you're named after a fruit, and you are so cute."

She looked at him with a giant fake smile on her face, then at Hubert and said, "Good morning, gentlemen. Giving classes again, Mr. Alexander?"

Everyone laughed except Clayton, as he tried to explain, "I'm sorry, baby, I am just not good with names. Can I offer you some gum or something," holding out a stick of Big Red.

"No, thank you, Clayton Lewis," looking at him, letting him know that she remembered his name. "Mr. Alexander has exactly what I want."

Hubert then reached in his desk, and pulled out a box of orange Tic Tacs, and handed them to Alisha, trying to avoid looking directly at Christina. "Good morning. We were just going over some requisition stuff. And how are you this morning, Ms. Douglass?"

"Can somebody introduce me to the new broad, please?" Clayton yelled out.

Alisha slowly answered, "Clayton, this is Christina Douglass, whose name you will soon forget, and, Christina, this is Clayton Lewis. He is also a trainee."

"Nice to meet you, Clayton," reaching out to shake his hand.

"C-Nice, and the pleasure is all mine."

"And, Mr. Alexander, I am doing just fine, a little nervous, but Ms. Coleman seems to be a great person to work with."

"That is wonderful, hard to believe, but wonderful," Hubert added, looking at Alisha.

"What, that I am doing fine?"

Leaving herself wide open Hubert replied, smiling, "Oh no, you are fine."

"Yes, baby, you are fine," Clayton added.

"No, it is hard to believe that Alisha 'Peaches' Coleman is a great person to work with," Hubert added.

"Come on, girl, let me introduce you to people around here that really matter. Thanks for the Tic Tacs," Alisha said after smacking her lips together. And with that, the two walk out, but not before Hubert took one more jab at Alisha.

"And, Ms. Coleman, if and whenever I give a class, I will make sure I send your boyfriend the memo," Hubert added with a *Take that* look on his face.

Alisha just rolled her eyes and she and Christina walk out, with Christina waving.

After the door was closed and Hubert and Clayton were alone, Clayton pounded his fist into his open palm and said, "Man, now that is one peach that I want to take a bite out of, and her trainee too."

"Only advice I can offer, my friend, is just be careful. She is a sweet girl on the outside, good heart, great intention, but, buddy, there is a monster that lives deep within, so be careful."

"I know that your game is tight and all, Hue, but I am good at what I do. EP told me the same thing, man, I am fresh out of college, not high school. I will be twenty-four next June."

With his hands up in surrender mode, "Okay, Clayton Lewis, Mr. C-Nice, do your thing, your way, like Burger King, just do not let it affect your job performance."

Clayton seemed to be back to himself now. "Why is it that everyone around here thinks they know everything?"

"No, C, it's not that," Hubert explained. "We are like a family around here, and certain things make families function, so we try to focus on those things that make the family run smooth. None of us are perfect, so we look out for each other. We try to be our brother's keeper, bear our brother's burdens, and whatever helps generally help the team, in turn keeps the family from becoming dysfunctional."

"Do you want to be some preacher or something?"

Hubert laughed, and quickly answered, "No, never that. I don't think that God wants me in that capacity."

"Whatever, preaching is preaching, whether it is godly or worldly. Someone trying to persuade you to make a decision, based on their perspective."

Hubert thought for a second, walked behind his desk, and answered, "That was deep, and I do have to leave in a minute, but I want to respond to your statement. I would say that godly wisdom not only makes you a better person, but it prepares you for the supposed afterlife. Worldly wisdom might make you street-smart or educated, but the person's perspective has to have truth. Godly wisdom is truth, so you cannot compare the two. So you want your decision to be persuaded by truth and knowledge and not perspective."

"That makes sense. You sure you're not going to be a preacher?"

Smiling, Hubert responded, "I am sure. But I have a meeting to attend. Do not forget to e-mail me the confirmation numbers."

Clayton walked out, seeing Hubert a little differently in his eyes now, shaking his head, thinking to himself, *That really did make sense.* Hubert was on his way to a meeting when he ran into Christina in the hallway.

"Hello, Mr. Alexander."

"Didn't I tell you to call me Hue?"

"Well, I am the new girl and this is my first day. I just cannot come in a building calling people in charge by their first names or nicknames, it is unprofessional."

"Ms. Douglass, I think you make a good point and I am going to leave it at that," pointing in the air, and starting to walk off.

Christina however added as Hubert was walking away, "But there are other names I could call you outside of these four walls, when work is done."

Hubert looked back, took a deep breath, exhaled and headed back toward Christina. "I have a meeting now. What time do you take lunch so we can clear the air of some things?"

As alluring as she could possibly say it, "I will be with Ms. Coleman all day, and probably take lunch with her. But I will be at the supermarket on Main at around five twenty-five when I get off, getting something from the deli. Maybe we can clear the air there, or do you have to be home at a certain time?"

Speechless for about thirty seconds, Hubert responded, "Are you propositioning me?"

"Mr. Alexander," she explained smiling. "Proposition you to do what, buy me a sub? If I propositioned you, you would not have to ask. Go to your meeting, sir."

Baffled but intrigued, Hubert could only say one word: "Wow." And as he walked off, that was the only word running through his head. He attended his meeting, performed all of his daily tasks, and the day was about to come to a close when Eric and Clayton walked in his office.

"So, are you going to hit the round table at the spot with us?" Eric asked.

"Let me make a phone call first." Hubert picked up the phone and called his wife, but she did not answer, so he left a message. "Baby, I hope you had a wonderful day, with those bad kids. I am going to run by DA's with the boys for a while. I will be home before seven. Call if you need me. Love you."

"Aw, that is so sweet. We are going to head on over. How long are you going to be?" Eric asked.

"I have to tie a few things up, I will be there shortly. Don't let your boy get drunk before we start."

As Hubert was preparing to leave, Alisha poked her head in the door. "We are leaving, so we will see you tomorrow."

"You're not going by DA's?" Hubert asked.

"I may, but I thought that 'honeymooners' could not get out yet," Alisha said with the quote-unquote fingers up.

"I may run by for a minute, I don't know."

"Okay, bye," ended Alisha as she walked off.

But right behind Alisha was Christina, and she simply leaned in waving and whispered, "Five twenty-five."

Hubert thought to himself for a moment, what could be the harm in just meeting with her to talk? He thought, nothing could happen in the grocery store. And even if someone saw him, he could have just been shopping for something. So he texted Eric from his cell phone letting him know that he will be at the club, but will be running a little late. He then jumped in his truck, did a quick look-over in the mirror, and made his way to the grocery store. When he got there, he surveyed the entire parking lot for known cars, and then took a spot in the crowded area to avoid suspicion. Again, he did a quick look-over in the mirror. As he was getting out of the truck, he looked around, and grabbed the closest shopping cart he could find, and pushed it into the store. It was now about five twenty-three, and as he was coming to the deli area, he noticed Christina already there, looking at him, smiling. He pushed the cart over to where she was.

"Hello, Mr. Alexander—oh"—covering her mouth—"excuse me. Hello, Huey."

"Just Hue, just Hue."

"So, are you hungry, or is the wife fixing a big plate for you?"

"No, I'm good, I don't know why I am here, or how long I am going to stay, but I guess I wanted to see how you acted outside of work," Hubert explained,

"Mr. Alexander," Christina said, smiling, moving closer. "Are you nervous? You seemed so calm and collected in the office." Now she was getting even closer to Hubert, that they are now almost face to face with their lips just about touching. "So in control, suave and smooth, now you seem all nervous."

Hubert whispered softly, "What is your angle, baby?"

"No angle, Huey, I just want to have some fun, and I heard from many sources that you were great at that. So were my sources false?"

"Peaches was telling you about the old Hue."

"I did not say that Peaches told me anything. So have you been with her?"

"No."

"You lie."

"I am serious."

"Okay, Serious, tell me what you want to tell me, but everyone knows, and I can tell from the first day. But I am all right with it." She looked at Hubert, and at the deli. "You know what, I am not hungry now. Is there a park, or somewhere we can just walk and talk for a few minutes? And I swear I will let you go home, I just want to talk for a while."

"No, but we can go to the school next door. There is a track behind the playground, and we can walk for a few minutes, because I promised the guys I would come by the club for a bit."

The two left the supermarket purchasing nothing, and drove off to the school next door in separate cars. Hubert drove up first and backed in, and she pulled up beside him and got out of her car. But instead of waiting to start walking, she walked over and got into the passenger's seat of Hubert's truck, laid the seat back some, and just stared at Hubert, and right then all Hubert could see was thigh, and she knew that he was watching it.

"Nice truck," she said.

"Thanks."

"Are you turned on by me, Huey?"

"Who wouldn't be?"

At that instant, Christina, got up on her knees in the seat, leaned across, and kissed Hubert on the cheeks, and looked at him for his next move. Immediately, they both go into a continuous, passionate kiss that seemed to be leading somewhere else. However, Christina stopped, smiled, licked her lips, only to return to her car and drive off. With his body still heated from the moment, Hubert decided that he was not going by the club, but going home to his wife. When he arrived there, he checked the mirror again to make sure he still looked proper, no hair or lipstick and that everything was appropriate, and as he was getting out of the car, he noticed that Shayla was leaving the house. He walked up to her, and embraced her, kissing her, telling her how he missed and wanted her.

"Hue, baby," was her response, pushing him away. "What has gotten into you today?"

"I want you."

"Baby, I want you too, and I know that your hormones are raging, but I have four more parent-teacher conferences that I have to oversee tonight."

"Can I get a quickie?"

"Yeah, as quick as I get back home. Aw, I am sorry, baby, but it is cute, though." She kissed him on the lip, and walked toward her car. "I am running late, be back by nine."

Needless to say, Hubert was a little frustrated, or maybe a lot frustrated. So he ended up going into the house, taking a shower and fixing him a drink, and waited for his wife to get home.

Weeks went by on the job, and he and Christina just spoke and smiled at each other but said nothing about the situation, until one day when they were both alone in the lounge.

"Hi, Huey."

"You're a mess, Ms. Douglass," Hubert said to her, pointing at her, walking out.

"No, wait, I am sorry." She paused for a moment, and slowly said, "I got scared."

"Here is the deal," Hubert started explaining in a very controlling manner. "My wife is chaperoning a field trip to DC on Thursday. This is what I am going to do. I am going to get a hotel room when I get off and I expect you to be there no later than five forty-three. If you come at five forty-four, I am not opening the door." She just smiled and shook her head, but gave no answer. This confused Hubert some. "So what do you think?"

"I told you that when you get in this building, you are just a control freak," she replied with her two hands scratching the air at Hubert. She then put her hands down and smiled, and responded, "But I like it, I will be there at five forty-three."

Hubert, thinking he had done something, just smoothly smiled and walked out of the office with his chest poked out, and then suddenly he heard Christina call him. He first looked around to see who was looking, but they were the only people in the hall. He turned around, and she looked at him with her arm with the watch in the air, and she asked, "Shall we synchronize our watches?"

Hubert just grinned, shook his head, and walked off.

Thursday finally came and the two did meet after work on time, and they enjoyed each other's company into the late hours of the night. This relationship would continue on to the point where it would really get out of control.

5

Out of Control

This relationship would go on for months, with some people speculating, some people knowing, and some people not even having a clue. They both would get very bold, meeting on the weekends, having dinners together, even to the point of having relations right in Hubert's office at work. They had both gotten in too deep, and were catching feelings, and feelings make you forget about what you are actually doing, who you are actually hurting. What started out as cheating or a simple fling now becomes a second relationship with expected behaviors, similar to the first and most important relationship: the wife. So the juggling act begins. At some point, someone will get disappointed, and eventually hurt.

On one occasion, Christina was mad at Hubert because he did not leave his wife to come and see her one evening. Hubert called her on the phone, wanting her to meet him so that they could talk about what happened.

"Hello?"

"What's up, Chris, what are you doing?"

"Nothing," she said very quietly.

"What's wrong?" Hubert asked, knowing exactly what was bothering her.

"What do you want, Huey?"

"Oh, it's like that now," Hubert answered in a voice like he was always in control. "I want to see you tonight."

Christina then answered sarcastically, "Why, is your wife busy?"

"I guess I deserved that one. So, can I see you or what?"

"All right, Hue, but not for long. I have some things to do tonight."

Hubert, not really caring about what she had to do because he had his own agenda, told her, "Well, I told Shayla that I was going to be out until at least one, and it is only seven thirty, so don't worry about what you have to do. Let's just relax, and enjoy each other's company until about twelve forty-five."

"I have to leave by nine thirty," reminding Hubert again that she had to leave early.

Still wanting to be in control, Hubert smiled, and told her on the phone, "All right, nine thirty. Meet me at our spot in about fifteen minutes," and hung up the phone. And he thought to himself, *I wish she wouldn't have me leave my house for just an hour and a half.*

They met at the spot, and Hubert asked her to come and get in the truck. Even though she was still a little upset with him, she still got up into the truck, looking at Hubert as if she wanted to hit him in the face with her purse. And they started to drive off.

Hubert looked at her with a charming smile on his face. "Are you mad at me?" he asked.

Not looking at him, she answered, "Hubert, right now, I am very confused, and I do not know." She then slowly turned to look at him, and posed a question. "Should I be mad at you?"

"Listen," Hubert started, but was quickly interrupted by Christina.

"No, Huey, should I be mad with you?"

Hubert put up his pointer finger, to begin explaining his side. "Chris, certain rules apply when you are having an affair. It is hard to get out of commitments that you were already obligated to. I am sorry that I could not be with you, and I missed being with you."

Christina stared attentively, nodding her head as Hubert spoke, knowing that he was going to try and prove something.

He went on explaining. "Baby, life is a game, and relationships are based on points."

She now stared a lot more confused now than attentive.

"When I met you, I was immediately interested, so without you even knowing, I was down one point. Come to find out, you were also interested, or at least intrigued. This evened our points out, which created a good chemistry, because no one was up any points."

She was now looking at him like he was crazy, but she let him continue without interruption, because she was very curious with where he was taking this conversation.

Hubert asked her, "We are having fun, right?"

She looked at him, but did not answer him. He reached over, and squeezed her thighs, tickling her. She tried not to laugh, but because she was ticklish it was very hard; so, smiling, she grabbed Hubert's hand, smacked it, and pushed it back to his side of the truck.

"Right?" he asked again.

Christina did not say anything, but, smiling, nodded her head yes. Hubert continued with his story.

"I made a mistake when I did not meet you, and you were upset with me."

"Were," Christina blurted out.

Hubert put one finger up, to stop her from talking so that he could continue. "As I was saying, before I was so rudely interrupted, you were upset with me, which changed the game. I was now down by two points because of anger, but the fact that you even got into my truck awarded me with one point."

He then pulled over into a parking lot, and started to play a one of their favorite love songs they enjoyed ever since they were together. He reached over, and grabbed her hand, and began to explain softly. "My mom was over, my wife's parents were over, my daughter and some friends were over. I am sorry. In any other predicament, I would have been there for you, and I promise that I will make it up to you."

After he said all of this, he kissed her hand and asked, "Do you forgive me?

She stared at him for a few seconds, smiled, and snatched her hand back from him. "I hate you!" She covered her face with both hands and, in an emotional manner, asked, "What are you doing to me?"

Hubert thinking that he was in pretty good shape, knowing that she did not mean that she hated him for real, questioned her again. "Do you forgive me?" He looked at her with a serious expression, waiting and anticipating an answer.

"Dammit, Hue, I forgive you!" she yelled. "But you know what? I am more upset with myself because I cannot be mad at you."

Hubert smiled, shaking his head, asked her, "You know what that means, don't you?"

"What?"

Hubert smiled, and after pausing for a second, told her, "It means that we are even again."

She tried to warn him, saying, "Don't get too cocky," but before she could get the word *cocky* out of her mouth, Hubert pulled her head over and gave her a long, passionate kiss.

Hubert eventually pulled back, and she seemed as if she still wanted more, with her lips still puckered and eyes closed. He moved back over to his side and, still smiling, leaned back in the driver's seat with confidence.

Christina opened her eyes and immediately asked, "I guess you think you are up one now, huh?"

Hubert just laughed, as she rolled her eyes at him, and shook her head.

"Are you hungry?" he asked.

"No, Hue. Actually, I have to get back to my car."

"So, I guess you are leaving me now?'

"No, baby, I told you that I had something to do."

He drove her back to her car, both of them smiling but neither saying a word. She then broke the silence, telling him, "I really do not want to leave, but I have to go."

Hubert, trying to be hard, told her, "You have to do what you have to do." In his mind, he never thought that she was really going to leave him that early.

He then leaned over, and gave her another long, passionate kiss, this time fondling her body, telling her softly in her ears that he did not want her to go, hoping to change her mind about leaving. She pushed him away, breathing hard, and after a strong exhalation told him, "No, Hue, I really have to go."

"Come on, Chris, I told Shay I was going to be out until at least one. Don't leave now."

Christina stared at him; one, because she had told him over the phone that she had to leave, and two, she was tired of hearing his wife's name. This made her upset after all of the kissing and pleading, that he would still make getting back to his wife seem more important. So to try him, she asked, "Spend the night with me, Hubert."

"You know that I can't do that."

"Well, let me out, please."

"So it is like that?" Hubert asked, still playing, locking her door from his side of the truck.

Christina was not in a playing mood, and yelled, "Hue, let me out of this damn truck!"

Hubert then got quiet, and hit the unlock button, shaking his head. Christina grabbed her purse, looking at Hubert like she wanted to say something. She opened the door, and stepped down, out of the truck, and as she was about to close the door, she told Hubert, "Go home to your wife, Hubert. Surprise her, treat one of us like we wanted to be treated tonight—no, treat one of us like *you* wanted to be treated tonight."

Christina walked to her car and left, never looking back toward Hubert's truck.

Hubert, with entirely too much time on his hands, decided that he still did not want to go home to his wife. So he ended up driving to DA's to see what was happening there. As he reached Donovan's, he sat out in the parking lot for a few minutes, wondering to himself, should he really go home, and why did Christina really leave? So, thinking like so many men do today—like so many people do, for that matter—he decided he would take a drink. As he entered the bar, he noticed Eric and Clayton sitting at a table, and when they noticed him they signaled for him to come over. So he told the hostess that he was going over to the table with his friends, and she walked him over and gave him a menu.

"What's up, boss?" Clayton asked.

"Chilling, man, just needed to get out the house for a while. What do you guys have going on?"

"Your boy E over here is sweating this girl in the purple at that table, but is scared to go and talk to her," Clayton explained.

Hubert looked over his shoulder to see the girl they were talking about. "Yeah, she is hot. Go holler at her, E, stop playing."

"I tried to tell him. Your mentor is here now, go on and impress him," Clayton added.

They continued pushing the shy Eric to go and talk to the young lady for a few minutes, when Hubert came up with a plan.

"Here's what you do," he started explaining. "Do you have your phone on you?"

"Yes," Eric answered.

Smiling and shaking his head as if he had a brilliant plan, "Now, turn your volume off and leave your phone over here, then walk over there like you are looking for your phone, and make it seem like the phone was right where she was sitting. Make eye contact, if she is interested, she will want to help you find your phone. Have her call your cell phone, to see if you guys can hear it ring. Remember, make eye contact, and after you do not hear it ring, thank her or thank them for that matter, and come back over here for further instructions."

Eric did just as he was told, and the young lady seemed very helpful; even the other girls were helpful. While she was calling Eric's cell phone, Clayton and Hubert were watching what took place, trying to be discreet. Eric did a great job, thanking the girls, and even looking under other tables on the way back to the table. Most importantly, he made eye contact, and she seemed interested.

"I did exactly what you told me to do, what's next?"

"Now did she seem interested?" Hubert asked.

"Yeah, she was, and her friend could tell too," Eric replied, smiling.

"Now, are you ready?"

"I am ready."

"Grab your cell phone and call her."

"Call her?" Eric asked, confused.

Instantly, Clayton picked up on what was going on, and yelled out with his fist on his mouth, "Oh snap! Playa, you just got the number. You a bad man, Alexander! That must be how you got that white joint on the job."

The table got quiet for a moment. Everyone looked around at each other, but Hubert was not in the mood to allow Clayton to mess up his night. "Calm down, Clayton, calm down, you gone make the man nervous," Hubert said, laughing. "Now go ahead and give her a call, and use this line: *Now that I have the number, am I lucky enough to get the name*. And let's just see what happens."

So Eric picked up his phone, and called the last number, and she picked up, while he watched her.

"Hello."

"Now that I have the number, am I lucky enough to get the name?" Eric asks nervously.

"Who is this?"

"My…my name is Eric, and I just came over looking for my phone."

Just then they made eye contact, and she just smiled, and pointed him out to her girlfriends, and they all laughed, and were giving high fives to each other. She then went back to the phone.

"All you had to do was ask," she said, "but that was unique."

Eric, with a little more confidence, asked, "So your name is?"

"Oh, yeah. Angela, Angela Carroll," she told him, laughing.

"So, Angela Carroll, would you like to meet at the bar, and maybe learn more about each other over a drink?"

"Sure, I will meet you there."

They made it to the bar, and they seemed like they had a wonderful time getting to know each other. Meanwhile, Clayton had walked over and started talking to one of her other friends, and he joined the new couple at their table, and Hubert was alone again waiting to order a drink. And just when the waitress arrived, one of Angela's friends came over, and asked to sit with him. She and Hubert sat and had drinks, Angela and Eric came over and they had drinks, all of the girls and all of the guys got together and had drinks, so by then Hubert was a little intoxicated. But not too intoxicated to notice Donovan in deep conversation with a guy that looked very familiar. At that time, one of the girls started massaging his neck, and he was really enjoying it. What happens: they end up in his truck, and back at her apartment, and the rest is obvious. All of this happened because Hubert was upset that his "girlfriend" did not want to spend time with him, so he figured he needed to hang out some more and have fun instead of going home to his wife.

After this point, Hubert had gotten out of control. Not only was he still in a relationship with Christina as well as his wife, but he was flirting with every attractive skirt he came across.

Days later, Hubert and Donovan were together in a department store. They were ready to check out when they both noticed the cashier. She was tall, dark-skinned, with long braids in her hair. She wore glasses, but looked extremely mean.

Donovan noticed her first. "Man, why is it that every time I come in here this broad is never smiling?"

The cashier had to come away from the counter to scan an item in a customer's basket, and Hubert caught a glimpse of her body. "I do know, man. She is probably looking mean because no one is taking care of her right," rubbing his hands together, smiling.

"Hue, leave that girl alone. Do you ever think you've had enough?"

"I just can't help it, man. She is sexy. And why do you have to say it like you're mad?"

"I'm just saying."

The two got to the front of the line, and as the cashier rang in their items, no one said a word. Donavan looked at Hubert, and Hubert looked at the cashier, and the cashier just looked mean. As Donovan paid for the items, the cashier thanked them both and told them to have a nice day. Donovan walked off, but Hubert stayed for a few seconds more.

"Can I help you, sir?" asked the cashier.

"I just wanted to tell you that, with all due respect, you have the perfect frame," Hubert answered, looking very serious.

The cashier actually smiled a little, looking into Hubert's eyes. "Thanks," she replied.

Hubert then walked out, but before he got to the door, he looked back to see if the cashier was still watching him. And certainly, she was still staring at him.

He caught up with Donovan. "Yeah, I will be back."

"What did you say to her?" Donovan asked.

"Nothing, Donovan, I just told her that she would look a lot better if she smiled."

"Yeah, right. She would have cursed you out! Your boy EP said he wants to do a round table at five today. Are you going to make it?

"What time is it now?"

"Four twenty," Donovan replied as he looked at his cell phone.

"Well, I'll just ride over to the club with you, and have Shay come pick me up from the club later. That way we can go by the house and see Nikki when I pick up my truck."

"So no major plans for tonight?"

"Man, even God had to rest," Hubert said as they both laughed.

At the club they met with Eric, Clayton, and a few guys from the job already sitting at the table. Donovan joined in.

"So, this is my first time at the round table. How does it work?" Clayton asked.

Hubert explained "Well, if there is something that has been bothering you for a while, or you have a question and you want to discuss it—it can be on the job or personal— we go around the table and look for responses. And if we agree that you have the best topic, everyone at the table has to weigh in. But we try to weigh in before everyone gets too drunk. Let me introduce everyone first, because I see a new face. I am Hubert, from J. Marshall Marketing. Also from J. Marshall is Clayton, Eric, Victor, and Latrell. This is Donovan, my good friend, and owner of the bar." Everyone spoke when Hubert finished introducing who he knew.

Victor, who worked in distribution at J. Marshall said, "This is my good friend, Robert Taylor. He works for the IRS, and is down to give some training, and he wanted to join us today."

"Well, welcome to the club, Robert, and to the round table," Donovan said. "I will have a pitcher come to the table every fifteen minutes, until someone seems drunk. And then I will make it every twenty minutes," Donovan added and everyone laughed. "So, who wants to start?"

"I know that I am new, but I want to start," Clayton yelled out. "My question is for Bobby, the IRS man." Everyone laughed except for Robert. "Why is it that we have a country that is trillions of dollars in debt, but they continuously run after people for a few thousand dollars, as they, the country, keep building new debt? Better yet, who was in charge when we were a billion dollars in debt, a million dollars in debt!"

"This man gets hyped, Robert, don't take it personal," Hubert responded.

Robert took a drink, and replied, "Even though this is not my department, I would like to respond to some of the questions. For one, sometimes we want something or get into something that we cannot afford. In this case, we have to borrow from somewhere, whether it is from ourselves or from other countries, for that matter. And as this debt builds, we continue to get into other situations. This goes for the country as well as personally. Unfortunately, the personal tax money is already spoken for. The rest is politics and what was important at that time, and this is not my field, but I feel your pain."

"Great response," Donovan added. "Anything else on this topic?"

No one wanted to respond, but only commended Robert on his answer.

"Yes, Robert, I would like to welcome you to the table and also tell you that you are going to fit in well," Eric said. "Also, can we talk about a payment plan for me?" The table filled with laugher. "No, just kidding, but I would like to go next. My topic is from my job. I am working on a baseball promo, and I am wondering why it is so much harder now to promote what was once considered America's greatest pastime."

Everyone was trying to talk all at once, and one could not understand what anyone was saying.

Donovan yelled out, "Time out, time out, order in the court! You know we are supposed to go in order by where we are sitting. Are you guys drunk already? Clayton, Hue, then Bobby—I mean Robert." Again everyone laughed. "Does anyone call you Bobby anyway?"

"No, they don't, but it's cool," Robert responds.

"All right, C-Nice, you can talk," Donovan directed.

"I hate baseball. I played softball when I was younger, and I want to get on a team out here just to have fun. But professional baseball seasons are entirely too long. There is spring ball, regular season, then there are the playoffs. This thing starts in February and can end in late October. That is ten months, who can stay focused that long? It is so boring to watch, and those are my comments. So how do you guys think I done?" Clayton asked.

"You did very well, C, but there are no perfect answers. Everyone has their own opinion, but you did a fine job expressing yours," Hubert responded.

Even though Hubert was serious, Donovan and Eric smiled at the way Hubert sounded when he answered Clayton. Clayton seemed to have gotten a little offended, and got up and said he was going to the bathroom. Everyone looked at Hubert.

"What? What did I do?" Hubert asked with his arms in the air.

"Mighty fine job, partner. That is what you should have said," Donovan said as the table burst out in laughter.

"Look, it was my turn. I know that this guy does not really care for me. So when he asked, I just responded, so I could go. No one else asks how they did. You need to check your boy instead of looking at me like I did something wrong," Hubert said, looking at Eric.

"Man, are you going to go?" Donovan asked. "We are talking about baseball. You drunk?"

"He just wants somebody to be drunk because he can't drink on the clock," Hubert said. "Now I done lost my train of thought, messing with you guys. Oh yeah, I remember. I totally agree with C-Nice. Not only is the season too long, but they play too many games. I think that it is a hundred sixty-two regular season games. That is crazy. I can see it being America's pastime when there is no TV, computers, or serious competing sports. But who can keep up with all those games? You can be eighty-one and eighty-one and make the playoff. And get this, basketball plays eighty-two regular season games, and that is too many to me. NFL plays only sixteen regular season games, a game a week. More people keep track of that, because the anticipation is much greater."

Clayton walked back to the table and took a seat, and everyone looked at Hubert as he looked at Clayton and continued. "So, to piggyback on what my man Clayton said, the season is not only too long, but has too many games."

"Robert," Hubert called out.

"I love baseball, and I agree with what all you guys are saying. But I also think that the game has been tarnished by steroids and overpaid players. Overall, baseball is a great game. That is all I have to say."

"Vic, it's on you," Donovan said.

"I have nothing to say, I do not watch baseball," Victor responded quickly.

"Latrell, what's the deal?" Donovan asked, smiling.

Latrell was more on the religious side; very soft spoken, did not drink or curse, and had no girlfriend. He just liked coming to the round table and voicing his opinions, which were usually strange.

"Well, even though I agree with you guys, my problem with baseball is totally different," Latrell started.

"Why does that not surprise us," said Eric as the others who knew how Latrell acted at the table laughed.

"No, now let me explain," he started again. "My problem is with the intentional walk. You pay a pitcher millions of dollars, and call them great. The minute a good hitter comes up—or if you are in a situation where you have players on base and a good hitter comes up—instead of trying to strike him out, you elect to send him first, with four bad pitches. Is your pitcher not good enough to strike him out? That is like allowing a kicker in football not to kick the extra point after the touchdown, just take the points, or just giving the guy the two points for the free throw in basketball because they are that good. No one knows the outcome in anything until you try. This sometimes makes the pitcher seem worthless to me whenever he intentionally walks anyone. And that is it for me."

"That is a good point, a point I never considered before. But you did a fine job, Latrell," Donovan jokingly added, and even Clayton laughed, looking at Hubert. "Well, I never liked baseball, and you guys make me like it even less. Next topic."

Just then Shayla walked in and came over. She touched Donovan on his head, speaking to him, and then walked over and gave Hubert a peck on the lips.

"Hey, everybody," Shayla said.

"For everyone that does not know, this is my lovely wife, Shayla," Hubert said.

"I did not even know you were married," Clayton said to Hubert with a deceitful look on his face. "But so nice to meet you, ma'am."

"Don't play, C, you were at the reception."

"Yeah, right. I was a little tipsy, man. I forgot. When you work around all those people at the job, you just do not know who is married, who is single, or who is married running around trying to be single," Clayton added, still with a meaningful smile on his face.

Not trying to pay him any attention, Hubert got up from the table. "All right, guys, you are going to have to continue without me. I have to leave. Make sure you guys let me know how everything turned out. Nice meeting you, Robert. Are you ready, baby?"

"How much have you had to drink?" Shayla asked.

"We have not been here long, so probably two glasses of beer."

Shayla looked over at Donovan. "Is he telling the truth?"

"Yeah, Shay, we started kind of late today, so he's good," Donovan answered.

"I just want to make sure, because he has to drive that truck home," Shayla said. "Nice meeting you guys."

So Hubert and Shayla left, while the others stayed at the round table in discussion. But before they could get back to their topics, Clayton blurted out, "Now why are you going to cheat on a fine wife like that?"

Latrell, who looked more shocked than anyone else, quickly asked, "Hubert cheats on his wife?"

"Wait, wait, wait, we are not having this conversation, guys. No, he does not cheat on his wife!" Donovan said, defending Hubert. "Number one rule of the round table, Clayton, C-Nice or whatever you want to be called. No one says anything at this table about another person not here that they would not repeat to that person. The purpose of the round table is to keep each other sharp as we get older, not to bring each other down. So if that is the attitude you are bringing, C, you may not be as welcome next time. We look out for each other here—iron sharpens iron, player. So are you with us or not?"

Everyone stared at Clayton until he eventually responded, "I am with you."

Everyone was quiet for a few seconds, when Latrell spoke up. "Do you know that the statement you made about iron sharpening iron comes straight from the Bible? In Proverbs twenty-seven, I think."

Donovan looked at Latrell with a very serious look on his face. "Who cares? Now I know I need a drink. Latrell got me in here quoting scriptures."

They all laughed and finished off the topics at the round table, and Hubert left and spent family time with his wife.

Hubert left work early one day, and made his way back to the department store where he and Donovan had been days earlier to see if that same cashier was there. She was there, still looking serious in the face, but dressed like she was going to the club. Hubert picked up something to purchase and made his way to her line.

"Hello, sir, how are you today?" she asked with that serious look on her face.

"Do you really want to know, or are you asking just for the sake of good customer service?" Hubert responded, smiling.

She looked at Hubert like she was so confused about whether she had heard him correctly. "Huh?" she asked.

Hubert laughed and asked, "Why are you so serious and looking all evil? You are a beautiful young lady with such a pretty smile. But every time I come in here, you look extremely mean. Your face looks so tight, like you have been drinking pure lemon juice. Did I do something wrong?"

She smiled, covering her mouth. "I'm sorry, it's not you. I just hate this job, and every day it is always something new."

"So why do you stay?"

"I don't know. This is actually my second job, and I need the money. I only work a few days during the week, and Saturdays and Sundays."

"So what do you do on those days during the week when you're off from here?"

"I'm taking classes at the community college to become an RN," she answered.

"Cute and ambitious, that is an awesome combination. So where is the man in your life while you are doing all of this working and studying?"

"Right now, I am too busy for a man. I don't need no distractions from no man," she replied, twirling her finger and rotating her neck.

Hubert didn't say a word for a few seconds, and the two just stared at one another. And suddenly he had a plan. "How about this, can I take you out for a drink later? Just a drink to ease your mind a little and allow you to enjoy some good company." Looking at her name tag. "So what do you think, Rachel?"

Rachel looked down at Hubert's wedding ring on his finger and frowned. "Aren't you married? What is your wife going to say?'

Hubert smiled smoothly and simply said, "Are you going to tell?"

"You are a trip," Rachel said, handing Hubert his receipt. "Have a nice day, sir."

Hubert was now in damage control central; he knew, by the conversation and the chemistry, that she was interested. He had to think fast, and this is what he was good at.

"Listen to me for a second. It's not like you have any more customers to wait on," he began. "I am not asking you to marry me, sleep with me, or become my baby's momma. I simply want to have a drink with you, laugh with you, and help my new RN friend relax. It will be fun, and baby, you look like you could use some harmless fun."

"And if I agreed, what would you tell your wife?" she asked, again rotating the neck.

"I am working on this new project, and it is going to be a late night. However, I will run home and pick up something to eat and head back to work. Go to bed and do not wait up for me." Hubert then shrugged his shoulders as if to say *That is how easy it is going to be for me to get out.*

"You got it all planned out, don't you?

"Well, I actually am working on a new project, just not tonight."

"So what is your name, and what do you do anyway?"

"Oh, excuse my manners," Hubert said as he reached his hand out to grab hers. "Hubert Alexander, marketing executive for J. Marshall Marketing, and you have the softest hands."

"Rachel Ward," she replied, smiling with a confident look on her face. "And everything is soft."

"Well, it has been very nice to meet you, Rachel. Your customer service has definitely been above average. I am hoping that it will extend into the evening. And I also hope that one day I will be the judge on what is soft or not," Hubert responded, pointing at her, smiling.

She smiled and then asked, "What kind of name is Hubert?"

"My daddy's. Why, you don't like it?"

"It's just different, nothing's wrong with it. I've just never met a Hubert."

"So, Rachel Ward, deal or no deal?

"Where?"

"There is a hotel on Fifth, and it has an excellent bar and lounge."

"Hotel, are you serious?"

"Rachel, it is quiet, has soft jazz music, and a real relaxed atmosphere," Hubert replied.

"And just how often to you go to this hotel?" Rachel asked.

"When I finished college, I stayed there while I interned at the marketing firm. Why are you so determined to make me out to be this player pimp?"

"Because you probably are."

"So, Rachel, are you coming out to play or what?"

"What time?" Rachel asked, smacking her lips together.

"Make it nine thirty."

"You better not stand me up," Rachel said with her meanest look yet.

"I will see you around nine thirty, and I am looking forward to it." Hubert left the department store and headed home. On his way home, he received a call from Christina.

"Hello, stranger," Hubert said, answering the phone.

"Stranger, you are the one that left early and did not tell anyone."

"You have been somewhat distant the last few weeks, so I have been trying to avoid contact at the job. I do miss you. But I know that there is something going on," Hubert implied.

"It hasn't been the same since that night I left you early. Hue, baby, it is not always going to be your way. Yes, I knew the situation before I got into it, but just like you can say no, I should be able to say no without your spoiled behind getting mad. I am falling for you, and I know that I shouldn't be. I can be me with you, sometimes, I can even be someone else. When I am with you it just feels so risky and exciting, but at the same time, it's comfortable. In the next couple of weeks, we are going to have to sit down and have a really long talk. I have some serious decisions to make, Hue."

Hubert, who was pulling in at his yard, noticed that his wife's car was home. He now had to get Christina off the phone. "Baby, if you only knew how I felt about you right now. You know that I am working on this important project on the job. Let's plan something for Monday night, okay? But I have to go."

"You always seem to have to go now," Christina answered, sounding sad.

"Monday, baby, make no plans. I will talk to you later, bye," Hubert said, quickly getting her off the phone.

"Bye, Hue," Christina said, sounding upset.

Hubert then got out of the car, and went into the house. Shayla was in the living room lying on the sofa, watching television. "What are you doing home so early?" he asked.

"Hello to you to, Hubert," she said sarcastically. "I had a half day, and I was tired, so I left when the kids left. Those kids were getting on my nerves these last couple of weeks. They don't know what they want to do with their future. Every small problem is so enormous to them right now. Every girl thinks she needs to date, every boy lying about who he's dating. If it is not dating, you are being bullied by someone. Whatever happened to the 'sticks and stones' theory? When did it become a priority for all these kids to start dating so early? No one wants to come and talk about education anymore. And what are you doing home so early?"

As Hubert walked over to Shayla, she began to sit up on the sofa. Hubert came and gave her a kiss on the lips, and turned her around and started massaging her shoulders.

"There, there, baby, it's all right. Kids are not like how we used to be. Everyone wants to be in a relationship. You see it on every television show, even cartoons. And so many parents are not sitting down with their kids, pushing education over relationships like ours did. They are so busy keeping up with the Joneses that peer pressure, music, and television are raising a lot of our kids today. It is sad, baby," Hubert said.

"That feels so good, Hue, don't stop," said Shayla, enjoying the massage. "And the one kid that does come into my office about college is so lost. He is on the football team, and he is trying to get into college. Mind you, it is too late. I told him months ago to fill out all of the paperwork, and take the SATs. He comes in today, and gives me the paperwork. I tell him, Ricky, you have to sign this. He says, I did. I told him, no, you printed your name. This boy tells me that he never learned to sign his name in cursive. So I asked him could he write in cursive, and he said not really. Hue, this may not be a big issue for you, but that is so disappointing for our school system, to have seniors that have not learned how to properly write. Even if it is sloppy, the third-grade teacher should have made him try. But here he is in the twelfth grade, Hue, and has to write his name in print on his paychecks."

"These days, baby, most people have direct deposit. All he has to do is remember his pin number," Hubert said, smiling.

Shayla then took her elbow, and hit him in the stomach. "You would not understand, Hue. And you never told me why you were home so early anyway."

"Well, while I am waiting on some important information for this new project, which should arrive later today, I figured I would come home, fix dinner before you got here. I wanted to spend a little time with my baby before I went back to work, because I know that it is going to be a long night."

"Aw, Hue, that's sweet. Are you also going to run my Calgon bath for me after dinner?" Shayla asked, still enjoying the massage.

"But of course, love, I got you," Hubert responded, smiling from within.

"So what's for dinner anyway?" Shayla asked.

"Chinese, baby, and it will be here in about thirty minutes after I order."

Again, Shayla elbowed him in the stomach as they both shared a laugh. The evening at home went as Hubert planned, and he was out of the house by 9:10 p.m. He made it to the hotel to meet Rachel. The lounge was really nice; perfectly lit, quiet music, and there were only about five other people in there including the bartender. Rachel was sitting at the bar, sipping on what seemed to be a glass of water as Hubert walked up and tapped her on the shoulder.

"Hello, my little night nurse, how are you?" Hubert asked with his hand on the back of her chair.

"I am all right. I see you got out of the house. I really thought that you were going to stand me up," Rachel said, smiling.

"You look cute tonight, with your hair all down. How could I ever stand you up?" Hubert then softly said but knew that she could hear him. "Shoot, stand you up, I am trying to think of a way to lay you down."

"You are a mess," Rachel said, smiling and rolling her eyes at the same time. "Are you always this straightforward?"

"That was just an opening joke to break the ice. Do you want to grab a table over in the corner?" Hubert asked.

"Sure," she responded, shaking her head, staring at Hubert.

"What are you drinking?"

"I don't know, I don't drink much. You order something for me," she added.

"Bartender, can I get a double shot of Tanqueray and tonic with a twist of lime juice, and can I also get a Long Island Iced Tea for the lady? We will be over at that table in the corner."

"Are you trying to get me drunk?" Rachel asked as they walked over to the table.

"Not a chance, baby. A drunk woman is no fun to anyone," Hubert explained as they sit down and he moved in closer to her, looking into her eyes. "I want to get to know you while you are sober and still smiling and looking beautiful." He then leaned in and kissed her on the cheek.

"You are so full of yourself," she said, smiling, as the bartender brought their drinks over and placed them on the table.

"Thanks, sir. I will probably order one more before I leave," Hubert said to the bartender, still staring at Rachel.

"Would you two like to see a menu?" the bartender asked.

Hubert, still staring at Rachel, "Are you hungry?"

"No, I'm good," she responded.

"No, thanks," Hubert said to the bartender as he finally took his eyes off Rachel. That was only for a few seconds. He again turned his attention back to Rachel. "Why do you say that I am full of myself?"

"Because you are," Rachel said as she took a sip of her drink. "This is really good. Great choice. You are that cute guy that always knows what to say to a woman. It is never about you, but always about her. Why, because you always have a backup plan. Am I lying?"

Hubert took a sip of his drink and looked at her for a few seconds quietly, and told her, "Yes, you are lying! For one, I do not think that I am cute, and two, I was attracted to you the first time I saw you, but it just so happened that when we started talking we clicked, and the rest is history. No backup plan, no nothing."

"All right, if you say so," she said, smiling. "So what does a marketing executive do anyway?"

"I direct all of the marketing that leaves the firm. I have the final say, so my job is very critical on every account.

I have an awesome team under me that does all of the research of the different products for different companies. After we research the product, we investigate and evaluate the competition. And with all of that information, we create slogans, logos, billboards, or commercials, and use every bit of the advertising media that we can, from the TV, radio, phones, Internet, and any means to promote this customer's product. It can be hectic, but it can also be fun."

"Wow, it sounds like a lot. And why do you keep looking down at your watch?" Rachel asked.

"I'm sorry, I didn't realize I was doing that. How is your drink?"

"It was good, but I don't want another one. So, do you have kids?" she asked.

"Yes, I have a daughter, from a previous relationship. What about you?"

"Oh, no. No time for them. Too busy trying to get me straight. Maybe one day, when I find the right man. But I don't think that he is out there for me," she said, looking seriously into Hubert's eyes.

"Why are you looking at me like that?"

Rachel moved closer to Hubert and kissed him on his cheek and softly whispered in his ear, "What do you want to do with me, Mr. Marketing Executive?"

Hubert looked at Rachel and back at his watch, and yelled out, "Bartender, check please!"

The next thing you know, the two were in an upstairs room getting it on. Once they were finished, Rachel, with her head lying on his chest, asked, "Did you think this was going to happen tonight?"

"I was hoping it would, but I didn't want to push it."

"You were pretty good."

Hubert had his eyes closed, and just smiled as if he knew that he was. It was so obvious to her. Rachel took her fist and punched Hubert in the chest. "You are so cocky, you make me sick!"

Hubert laughed. "What did I do now? You were good too, baby. And I am not cocky, I am confident. Doesn't the Bible say, 'Cast not away therefore your confidence, which hath great recompense of reward?'"

"But, like, doesn't that have to do something with your confidence that God is going to help you get through?" Rachel asked.

"I don't know, it just works for me," Hubert said, smiling.

Rachel then got up and started quickly putting her clothes back on, saying nothing. Hubert just watched as she gathered all of her things and headed for the bathroom. She later came out, and looked over at Hubert, and finally said something. "I try to go to church every Sunday, and I know that I am not perfect, but when I know that I am in bed with a married man, and we are talking about the Bible, it is time to go. I'm sorry, it's not you, it's me." She rubbed down her face with both hands, and looked over at Hubert one more time. "I got to go." She left.

Hubert, wondering what had just happened, got up out of the bed, put his clothes on, and went home.

6

Caught

Early one Saturday morning, Hubert awoke to find several missed calls and voice messages on his cell phone. As he started going the phone, he noticed that all of the messages were from only two people: his boss and Christina.

He decided to walk into the bathroom with the cell phone, hoping not to wake Shayla, who was sound asleep. When he walked into the bathroom, he immediately turned on the shower to avoid any suspicions, and started listening to his voice mails. The first was from his boss.

"Hue, we really need to talk, call me when you get a chance, it is very important."

Hubert made a face, thinking to himself that something must be wrong at work. He then listened to the second message, which was from Christina. In this message, she paused for about six seconds before saying anything, but he could hear her crying in the background like she was trying to get herself together.

"Huey, I am so sorry, you are going to hate me, I am so sorry."

Before listening to any of the other messages, Hubert, scratching his head, now extremely puzzled, decided to go ahead and take a shower first, and deal with the messages with a fresher mind.

After a long, hot shower, Hubert started drying himself off, when he was interrupted by the soft voice of Shayla calling his name, and from the sound of her voice, something did not sound right.

"Yeah, baby," he answered.

"Open the door, Hue."

When Hubert opened the door, there was Shayla looking furious in the face, holding the house phone.

"What's wrong, Shay?"

"Check the phone message, and you tell me what is wrong."

"What's wrong, who called?" Hubert asked looking both scared and curious.

Seeming very frustrated, Shayla grabbed Hubert's hand and smacked the phone in his palm, yelling, "Check the message!"

Hubert took the phone and began dialing the numbers to check messages. The first message was his mother reminding him about Communion Sunday being the following day, and how she really wanted them there. After listening to that, he looked at Shayla, shrugging his shoulders, but the next message was truly a shocker for him. It was not his mother this time, nor a bill collector, or anyone he actually knew. The message said, "Hello, Mrs. Alexander, I just wanted you to know that your husband is sleeping with my wife. I know that you do not want to believe this, and neither did I, but I have all the proof that you need."

"What!" Hubert screamed in disbelief.

"*What?* Is that all you can say—*what?*" Shayla asked with one hand on her hip, and the other pointing.

"Who is this?"

"Naw, you tell me who it is, or better yet, who she is? I can't believe you, Hue." Shayla stormed out of the room, only to return seconds later. "I am not even going to ask you if it is true, because that stupid guilty look on your face immediately gave it away!"

With tears of anger, frustration, and hurt, Shayla walked up and got face to face with Hubert. "You chose this," she said, "I am leaving you!" She again stormed out of the bedroom, again only to return in seconds. "You know, Huey, I see how you look at those little biddies, but I pay it no attention, because I am secure with mine, but—"

Not able to finish her statement, she sat on the bed crying, with both her hands on her face. Hubert walked and sat beside her, and placed his hand on her shoulder.

"Don't touch me," she yelled. "I am so hot with you"— rubbing her eyes—"I am so hot with you. I see you look at other women, but it never mattered, that is normal. But to sleep with one of them! Not just any one of them but a married one at that. So because you can't control your stupid biology, you have not messed up not one family but two!" Looking very serious in the face, wiping the tears away. "For real, Huey, I want you to put some clothes on, pack some clothes, and leave right now or I am going to call the police and they are going to make one of us leave." She threw her hands in the air. "I can't believe this! Right now, Hue, I don't even want to hear what you have to say. So you can rehearse it, lie about it, or even deny it, but what you can do right now is get out!" Shayla then walked into the bathroom and slammed the door.

Hubert was still sitting on the bed, rubbing his forehead in a thinking position. He stood up, walked to bathroom door, and just when he was ready to knock, he changed his mind. He started putting on his clothes, packed a few things, and prepared to leave. After he was sure that he had everything and before he walked out of the door, he decided to walk back into the bedroom, where he saw Shayla now on the bed wrapped in a towel with the phone in her hands.

"Who are you calling?" he asked.

Shayla ignored him as if he were not even in the room.

He tried again. "When do you want to talk?"

With tears streaming down her face, she turned away from him to make it known that she did not want to talk to him. Hubert then walked out of the bedroom and out of the house, and got into his truck. Shayla, on the other hand, burst into a loud cry and lay across the bed, wondering what she had done to deserve this.

As Hubert started driving off, he now contemplated on whether to call Christina or his boss first. Thinking that he was not ready to deal with any more personal relationship stuff yet, he decided to call his boss first. "Top of the morning to you, sir," he started the conversation.

"Good morning, Hubert. How are you?"

"I have had better mornings, sir. What is on your mind on a Saturday?"

"Well, Hubert, I have had better mornings myself. Hubert, are you sitting down?"

"I am in the truck, sir. What is your story, boss?"

"Hue, how many times have I told you to be careful with those women in your life?"

"Several times, sir, why do you ask?"

"Apparently you never listened."

"Now you are really starting to scare me, Mr. Marshall. Did you by any chance talk to my wife?"

"Your wife, Hubert? This is not about your wife."

Hubert, already feeling in hot water, did not want to mention what was going on between him and Shayla back at home, so he just did not respond, and waited to hear what his boss had to say.

"No, Hubert, but remember when I told you that my son and his wife were having problems, and my wife and I left for Michigan to help them if we could? I told you that his wife wanted time apart, and he did not think that they needed it."

"Yes, I remember this."

There was a long pause in the conversation.

"Sir?" Hubert asked.

"Hubert, Christina Douglass is my daughter-in-law. She dropped the last name so that no one would know that I was giving her a job. Damn, Alexander, how could you?"

Completely speechless, Hubert pulled off on side of the road with one hand over his mouth, breathing intensely but saying nothing.

"Hue? Are you there, Alexander?" Mr. Marshall called.

After getting himself together, Hubert answered, "This can't be true."

"Yeah, buddy, you put me in a pickle behind your little pickle, and I do not say that with a smile on my face."

"I am so sorry, sir."

"It is always about this image you have to try and uphold for your friends. Life is not about an image, Alexander, it is about trying to do what is right. Try upholding that image one day!"

"Mr. Marshall, I am so sorry."

"Alexander, what does sorry help now? You are like a son to me, but you are not my son. My actual son is now so irate that he is now threatening to sue my company for allowing a management employee to get sexual favors from his wife, who was also an employee. Alexander, that is fraternization, and you know how the world looks at that now!"

"So what's next?" Hubert asked, holding his breath.

"Alexander, Monday morning I am going to need a letter of resignation from you on my desk, or Monday evening I am going to have to let you go. The choice is yours, and I hope that you make a better choice on this than you have been making in other things."

"You're firing me, sir?"

"No, Hue. You are a sum of your choices, so I expect that paperwork on my desk first thing Monday morning, and for that, Hubert Alexander, I am sorry for your family."

Hubert sighed in total disbelief, wondering to himself, could this be a dream, could he actually be losing his family and his livelihood all in a matter of hours? Hubert sadly told his boss, "I will have it on your desk first thing Monday morning."

"Good–bye, Hubert, I wish we never had to have this conversation."

Not responding, Hubert just closed his cell phone, ending the call.

Still parked on the side of the road, he thought hard about whether to call Christina. He picked up the phone, scrolled down to her name, but before pressing call he instead called Donovan.

"Yo," Donovan answered.

"You up, man?"

"Yeah, playa, what's the deal?"

"I gotta come through, man."

"What's going on?"

Hubert paused, not even understanding the emotion that he was feeling, but with his voice cracking and his eyes watering, he responded, "Everything is messed up, man."

Donovan sensed that something was very wrong. "What did you do, man?"

From that response, Hubert did not know if he really wanted to go over to Donovan's feeling like he felt. "You know what, man, I may just ride around for a while."

"You got me up, and now you got me worried, Hue, so if you don't come over here, I am coming to find you, so I will see you when you get here."

Before he could finish his sentence, Adrian grabbed the phone from him and in a soft, worried, motherly tone asked, "How are you, Huey?"

Trying to be strong to avoid questions from her, Hubert responded, "I am good, and yourself?"

"Don't front, Hue. I talked to Shayla already, and I am so not happy with you right now."

He could hear Donovan in the background. "What is going on, baby? Somebody had better tell me something before I start swinging!"

Joking with Donovan, Adrian said, "Aw, you are going to swing at someone with those cute pajamas on, I think that is so cute."

Reaching for the phone, Donovan asked again, "What is going on?"

"I will let Hue tell you when he gets here," she told Donovan. "Hue, it is going to be all right. We will see you when you get here."

"Adrian," he called out.

"Yes?"

"I don't want Nikki to know about this."

"Gotcha, Huey, I promise you she will not know a thing."

"Thanks," Hubert said as he closed the phone.

Now even though Donovan did not know what was going on at the time, he was aware that Hubert was sleeping with Christina, but "man law" would not allow him to tell his girlfriend about other friends' affairs when they were mutual friends with both parties. So as Hubert walked into the house, Donovan met him downstairs while Adrian was still upstairs, and after the hug and pound, Donovan pulled him to the side, and asked, "Did you get caught?"

"Long story, my friend."

In an almost silent lip-reading voice Donovan whispered, "Which one?"

Again Hubert's response was the same. "Long story, my friend, long story."

"Hey, Daddy, what are you doing here?" Nikki asked coming downstairs, giving her dad a big hug.

"Hey, big girl, I just wanted to hang with Donovan for a minute. Is that all right with you?" he asked smiling.

"Yeah, I guess that is cool."

"Where are you going this morning anyway?"

"Mommy is taking me to breakfast, being you and Uncle Don are hanging out this morning."

At the same time, Adrian was walking down the stairs looking at Hubert with an *I am still mad at you* look on her face. She walked to him, hugged him, and whispered in his ear, "I am still upset with you, but I am going to let you have your man time with Donovan. But we do need to talk."

"I know," Hubert replied. "You guys enjoy your breakfast, and don't eat too much."

They both laughed, and walked toward the door. Donovan held the door, and Nikki walked out first, saying, "Bye, Uncle Don."

Then Adrian walked by, giving Donovan a peck on the lips. "You had better take good notes, and tell me everything later."

"Enjoy your breakfast, baby," Donovan said, smiling.

Adrian walked to the driver's side of the car, looking back at Donovan, and before she got into the driver's seat, she yelled, "Everything." She and Nikki then drove off.

Back in the house, Donovan looked at Hubert, shaking his head. "Come on, man, come sit in the den. Do you want anything to drink?"

In his own world, Hubert did not respond.

"Do you want something to drink, man?"

Hubert, now following him into the den, answered, "Oh, I'm sorry, man. Get me a gin and tonic with a twist of lime juice."

Looking at him like he was crazy, Donovan replied, "First of all, man, you are not at the club, and second, it is ten o'clock in the morning."

"Yeah, you're right. Skip the tonic and lime juice, just give me a double shot of gin straight."

"Wow, well, let me fix you this drink, and get me some orange juice, and you can start talking whenever you want. Cool?"

"Cool."

While Donovan was in the kitchen, Hubert's phone vibrated. It was Christina. He really did not want to answer the phone, but he figured, what else could go wrong?

"Hello," he answered.

"I know that you hate me, and you probably do not want to talk to me, and I am sorry. But I want to see you."

"Chris, what do you want to see me for? Your husband ruined my life."

"No, I ruined your life," she started to explain, crying. "You made me feel like the woman I wanted to feel like. Every time that I wanted to tell you who I was, I thought that I would lose you, and I was not prepared to lose you."

"Look, I can't talk right now."

Still crying on the phone, "Hue, I'm leaving today to go back to Michigan, and I just want to see you, if only for a few minutes, if only for a few seconds. If only you knew how bad I just want to see you."

Hubert began shaking his head, holding the phone, looking down. "I'm at Donovan's. I will call you as soon as I leave."

Still crying on the phone, Christina answered, "Thanks. I will be waiting to hear from you."

Hubert hung up and hung his head down, not aware that Donovan was looking at him the entire time. "Here's your drink. Pick your face up, man, and tell me what's going on."

"Man, I got hemmed up."

"I figured that, but by who?"

"Christina."

"The white broad?"

"Yep, that's the one."

"Wifey found out?"

"Man, it goes so much deeper than that," Hubert said, leaning back in his seat.

"Wait, man, I think I might need a drink. Let me mix some vodka in this orange juice, and then you can finish, because this is getting deep, playa." Donovan got up and fixed a drink, and sat back down.

Hubert continued, "Are you ready for this, man?

"I hope," he responded.

"This joint is Marshall's daughter-in-law."

"Man, get the—!"

"Yep, and get this, Marshall asked for my resignation on his desk by Monday."

"You are lying, Hue, is that legal?"

"Her husband, Marshall's stepson, is a lawyer, and he came up with some lawsuit, stating that Marshall's company allowed a management employee to use their powers for sexual favors from his wife, or some mess like that."

"Oh, snap! So you are out of a job?"

"That is not all. This cat actually left a message on my house phone telling Shayla that he thought that she needed to know that his wife was sleeping with her husband."

"Man, I am going to need another drink," Donovan said as he jumped up and went to the bar. "You ready for another?"

Hubert shook his head no, still sipping on the gin, looking at his cell phone, when he noticed that Donovan was also shaking his head, but smiling real hard, making his drink.

"What the devil are you smiling like that about at a time like this?" Hubert asked.

Donovan sat and took a few sips of his drink, still smiling, and says, "I know that you do not want to hear this, but this dude thought this thing through. Look, he could have confronted you, beat you up—or got beat up, probably—he could have done something to your wife or his wife and gone to jail probably, but he chose to get you where it hurt—your family and your pockets. I am mad at him because you are my boy and he is trying to destroy you, but I will admit his retaliation game is tight."

"Thanks, Donovan, that helps a lot," Hubert responded, sipping his drink and staring at Donovan.

"Man, I don't know what to say. You're the man with all the answers, remember? All I can say, my brother, is whatever you need I got you. More importantly, how is Shay? That had to have been a hard pill to swallow for her."

"I don't know, buddy, she told me leave and that she did not want to talk. She is hot," answered Hubert.

"Rightfully so. You cheated on her!"

Hubert looked up at Donovan, and just stared at him for a few seconds almost in disbelief, and asked, "Why did I come over here again?"

Donovan laughed and took Hubert's empty glass and poured him another drink. He took the remote and turned on some music. "Man, you know I got you and I love you, but you have to know that if you play them games, you win those awards. Look at how long you ran married, look at how long you ran before you got married, look at how you ran in college." Donovan fixed Hubert's drink and came back and sat beside him. "Hue, you got a baby by my girlfriend. When you run all your life, Hue, the odds of getting caught are greater. The question is, how do you handle getting caught? Do you fix things at home? I know that you have to get another job and start over, and that is going to be tough. What happens with this

Christina chick? And even more important, do you stop running now?"

Hubert again looked over at Donovan, shaking his head.

"What, man?" Donovan asked.

"I know that with all of this mess going on this morning alone, you did not just bring up the fact that I have a daughter by your girlfriend?"

"Naw, man, that was just speaking to your running track record. I did not mean anything by it. Besides, after that didn't I pose some good questions for you to ponder?" Donovan answered, smiling.

"No, I did not come here for questions, Don, I came for answers."

The two sat taking sips of their drinks, quiet for about forty-five seconds. Then Donovan looked at Hubert with an innocent look on his face and simply, quietly said, "Oh." The two stared for a few more seconds as Donovan finished, "You mad at me?"

The two burst into laughter with Hubert shaking his head. "You see, this is why I do not have men friends."

After the both of them finished their laugh, it was back to reality for Hubert. He sat there in despair, contemplating what his next move would be. Would he actually go and see Christina? When would he talk to Shayla? What was he going to do about a job? And, above all, what was his mother going to think when she found out? He sat with both hands over his face, and leaned back in the seat.

Donovan looked at him, not knowing what to say or do. He did not want to offer him another drink, because one more would put him on the verge of intoxication. So here was Hubert confused about what to do, and Donovan confused about what to say. They listened to the music in silence for minutes, with both of their heads nodding to the beat.

"Look, I think I am going to see Chris for a few minutes before she leaves, just to hear what she has to say. She is leaving, going back to Michigan today, so at least I know that that part of my life is over, I guess. Then I will check into a hotel, and I will probably call Shay and my mother from there. So I am going to get with you later." Hubert then finished his drink, and headed for the door. "What were your plans for the day anyway?"

"I am going to be at the spot from about three to two, depending on business, unless Adrian has something else planned. But she will probably go and be with Shay later. I have nothing planned. Are you going to be all right? You know I have an extra bedroom?"

"I'm pretty good right now. And as for me resigning, I think they have to give me some kind of severance, and I have a 401(k), so I think I'm good for about a year at least, with all of these bills. So I know I'm good for the next couple of days, thanks. Besides, I do not want Nikki thinking that her daddy sucks, so I have to be careful with what she sees. But I'm good. Thanks anyway."

The two walked to the door, shook hands and hugged, and Hubert headed for his truck. Donovan yelled out, "When you do need me, I have an investment to tell you about."

Hubert threw up his hand for not being interested. "Oh Lord, not some more multilevel marketing mess! I get with you," Hubert responded as Donovan laughed and went back into the house. Hubert grabbed his cell phone to call Chris and set up a meeting place.

"Hello?" she answered.

"Hey, do you want to just meet at the school we met at when all of this started, or can you still get away?"

"That will be just fine. He has already left, and I am leaving in two hours."

"Are you in a hurry to get home to the hubby?"

"Hubert, after talking to you…I'm sorry, but I don't think that I want to see you now."

"All right, what is with you? You called me earlier saying that you wanted to see me so bad, but now you do not want to see me. What's the deal, Chris?"

"Can you answer a question for me?"

Now seeming upset with the world, he practically yelled, "What, Chris?"

"Never mind."

"No, ask your question."

"Remember that night you asked me to stay with you and I told you that I had something to do? Andrew…" She paused. "My husband called and said that he was flying in, and he just wanted to talk. So I told him that would be all right, and that is why I had to leave."

"Okay. And your question."

"Hubert, his flight was cancelled, and as mad as I was with you that night, I still wanted to see you. I was hoping that you did not go home. Hubert, I went by the club and there was some girl massaging your back, and I saw you take her out to your truck, I saw you leave together. I left hurting after that, but one question stayed in my mind. Did you do that because you were mad at me, or did you do that simply because that is what you do? Is that what your wife always has to go through, does there always have to be another woman? You are one of the most charismatic, one of the most interesting men I have ever met. You know what to say, you know what to do, you make me laugh, you can talk on any level, but you are a complete jerk due to a lack of commitment to relationships. My husband has many flaws because his work is more important than I am sometimes, but at least I know that his commitment is to one woman, and that is a lesson you can take from him. I know that I said that I had a question for you, but I just do not feeling like crying anymore, so, Mr. Alexander." There was a pause as she was trying to hold herself together, but he could almost hear the sob in her voice. Once she'd gotten herself together, she cleared her throat, and ended the conversation with,

"So, Mr. Alexander, this is good-bye." She then hung the phone up, and Hubert was in shock.

He set the phone down, and drove up to the nearest decent hotel but he could not check in until three. He decided to go and get some breakfast to feed the alcohol he had been drinking, but could only stare at the food. When he was able to check into the room and got himself situated, he knew he had some phone calls to make. The first person he decided to call was Shayla. She would not answer the phone after several tries. He only left one message, not apologizing, but asking whether it was all right for him to come by and get a suit for the next day's church service. He thought about what he did later that day, but after the few early morning drinks with Donovan, he decided he would take a nap, only to be awakened less than an hour later, by his cell phone vibrating on the table. He jumped up hoping it was Shayla, but it was his mother.

"Hey, Ma," he said rubbing his eyes.

"Hubert Alexander, what have you gone and done?"

"Ma, I messed up, and I have to fix it some kind of way. I know Shay told you what she knows, or thinks she knows, but she does not know that I lost my job too."

"Lost your job?"

"Yeah, Mom, the girl worked for me, and—ah, it is a long story, Mom, and I do not feel like talking about it right now."

"Hubert Alexander, I told you being alienated from God means being susceptible to the devil's will, and honey, you can't control what you do, boy! How many times do I have to tell you? Your daddy was the same way, rest his soul wherever it is."

Hubert, knowing this was the conversation that he was going to get, paid little attention. "Mom, I understand all of that, but right now, I have a situation at hand and I have some thinking I have to do. But, Mom, I will be in church tomorrow."

"That is where you need to be. Do not just come, you need to come and give your life, and not just be a hearer but a doer of the Word. You know—"

"Look, Ma, I am going to have to go," he said, interrupting her. "I promise you I will be there tomorrow for the eleven o'clock service. Bye, Ma."

"God bless you, son."

He then decided to try Shayla once again. This time she did pick up.

"Hello, Hubert."

"Hey, Shay, how are you?"

"What do you want?"

"I need to come over and get a suit. I promised my mother I would go to church tomorrow. And, Shay—"

Interrupted. "What, Hue, what do you want?"

Swallowing before he spoke. "Words cannot express my apologies, and I know that I messed up, but I do love you."

Interrupting again, "Hubert, is there something else important that you want to say."

"Shayla, I lost my job today too."

"Hubert, how do you lose your damn job on a Saturday? You know what, you don't even have to answer, I guess it had something to do with the girl you slept with." With her voice cracking, she said in an angry tone, "Huey, you disgust me. I will be out of the house until at least ten, come and get your clothes, and be out by the time I get home. As much as I loved you, I do not think that I want to see you right now." Crying on the phone, she ended with, "Bye, Hue," and hung the phone up.

"Shay. Shay!" Hubert yelled into the phone, realizing he was just hung up on. Very frustrated, he grabbed the phone and held it like he was going to throw it at the mirror, but he saw the reflection of himself. He came to his senses about breaking his phone or the mirror, and put the phone down and took a seat on the bed. He then called Eric to let him know what was going on.

"Hubert, what's up, player," Eric said answering the phone.

"Too much on my end, my friend. How are you making out?"

"I am chillin'. What's on your agenda for today?" Eric asked.

"Yo, E, is your boy around you?"

"Naw, he stepped out for a while. What's up?"

"Look, man, I do not want you to hear it from anyone else. I am resigning Monday morning."

"What?"

"Yeah, things got a little ugly with Chris. Turns out, her name is Christina Douglass Marshall. E, she is Marshall's daughter-in-law. She was having problem with her husband, Marshall's stepson, so she came down here to get away from him. She came to let her hair down for a while. So now her lawyer husband is threatening to sue his father's company. Marshall is furious, so lo and behold, I am out," Hubert explained.

"Wow, man, you all right?"

"I will be, but get this. Her husband even called Shay and told her that I was sleeping with his wife."

"Oh my goodness, bro. You are really in a bind. What are you going to do?" Eric asked.

Wanting to sound positive for his boy, Hubert responded, "Remember I told you a while back, that if it is true you have to eat it? Trust me, it does not taste good in the beginning, but I have to deal with it. I will be fine eventually."

"Well, do you need anything?"

"No, E, I am good for now, but thanks for asking. Monday morning, and the rest of the week, the rumors are going to start flying like vultures seeking decayed meat. Do not allow yourself to get caught up in it. Answer what you want to answer, defend what you want to defend, but whatever you do, do not get caught up in that mess. Peaches will probably be promoted, so just pay attention to details, like you did for me, and you will move up too."

"Thanks for the advice, but I am still trying to absorb this, Hue. It just does not seem right. Are you sure that there is nothing that you can do?"

"It is what it is, E. I guess it is just time for a new season. One last thing, before I have to go, keep a close eye on your boy."

"Wow, man, unbelievable."

"E, I will still be around. I will still be at the round tables hopefully. You can't keep a good man down."

"All right, I will see you around then," Eric answered as the two got off the phone.

Hubert, sitting on the bed, looked in the mirror, thinking to himself, if only he was as confident as he sounded on the phone with Eric. He shook his head in disbelief at what was going on in his life. He took a long shower, and tried to get another nap.

After about an hour, the phone rang again. Hubert reached over and grabbed the phone to see who was calling. It was Donovan. Hubert's first thought was not to answer, but he figured that Donovan would just keep calling. "Hello," Hubert answered, sounding like he was in a deep sleep.

"What's up, Hue? Just calling to check on you, man, to see how you are making out."

"I'm good, just resting."

"Where are you anyway?

"I'm good, Donovan. Why do you need to know where I am?" Hubert asked curiously.

"Are you by yourself?"

"Yeah, I am by myself."

"Man, I am just worried about you and Shay, and I know how you get when you start drinking, so I had to ask," Donovan responded, defending his question.

"Donovan, another girl is the last thing on my mind right now."

"I'm just saying."

"Did Adrian get you to call?" Hubert asked.

"Naw, man, what does this have to do with her? Can't I just want to call and check up on my boy when I know that he is in trouble? Does it always got to be Adrian's idea or your idea if it is a good idea? What do you—?"

"Donovan, what's wrong with you, man? You sound like my mom rambling on like that. I'm sorry, man, I just have a lot going on right now. So what did Adrian say about talking to Shay?"

"That she was hurting and talking out of serious anger. She said that she does not want to see you ever again. She mad, man," Donovan said.

"Wow, I really messed this one up. I have to fix it somehow. I am going by the house to talk to her tonight."

"Man, don't! Not right now. Give it a moment to marinate. Adrian says she's hot! Let her cool down some, bro. You did some jacked-up mess that had a domino effect on both of your lives. Adrian told me that Shay said that she does not even care about the house, the cars, her job or anything around here right now. Let her cool down some, bro," Donovan pleaded.

"Yeah, I guess you're right. She said she would be out until ten, so I had better go ahead and run by there and get my suit."

"Suit?"

"Yeah, my mom asked me to come to church tomorrow. I figured I had better go this time, or I will never hear the end of it."

"So I take it that she knows?" Donovan asked.

"Yeah, I guess Shay called and told her."

"Yeah, you are right, you had better go to church tomorrow. You may need to sing in the choir," Donovan added, laughing.

"You are right," Hubert responded, laughing. "Let me get myself together and go pick up these clothes, man. I will talk to you a little later."

"All right, playa. But are you sure you're good?" Donovan asked.

"I'm good, man, thanks for looking out."

"And, Hue."

"Yep?"

"Remember, let her cool down some, bro."

"I got you, man. That's why I am going over there before she gets back."

"All right, man, I'm out. Call me after church."

"No problem," said Hubert, and they both hung up.

Hubert got ready, and headed home. As he entered the driveway, he was hoping to see Shayla's car. But the driveway was empty. Hubert went into the house and grabbed his suit. Upon leaving, he noticed that the mirror in the bedroom was broken, and he looked at the floor, and noticed that the house phone was broken too. Hubert thought to himself, *Maybe Donovan was right. I had better let her cool down some.* Before Hubert left, he got the broom and cleaned up the glass and the pieces of the broken phone. When he went to throw the glass in the trash, he saw a phone number written on a piece of paper. It was Christina's husband Andrew's number. So now Hubert was wondering if Shayla had actually talked to him, and just what had he said if they did talk. Now scratching his head, Hubert looked down at his watch to see how much time he had. He noticed that he had time before Shayla got home, so he decided to go downstairs and fix himself a drink. While fixing the drink, Hubert looked up the wall at an eight-by-ten photograph that he and Shayla had taken a few years ago. He stared at the picture, sipping his drink and shaking his head. Hubert then walked out to the truck, put the clothes in the backseat, and got behind the wheel. But before starting the truck, he got out, went back into the house, and took the picture from the wall and left with it.

7

The Sermon

Hubert got up, got dressed, ate the little complimentary breakfast, and started making his way to the Sunday church service. He really just wanted to get out of that hotel room. He did not sleep well the night before. He had thought about staying at his mother's, but he really was not in the mood to hear his mother talk about who or what made him do what he had done.

There were usually two services—one at eight, and one at eleven. As expected, most people made it to the eleven o'clock service. It was also the service with the most excitement. There was more music, normally more people, and, most of the time, more talking.

Hubert arrived at about a quarter to eleven to get a good seat, but with the way church services were now, one could actually get there at any time—at least, some people believed that. Like most mornings, the same people got there early, and the same people got there late. Hubert was wondering whether Shayla would be there, considering she had already spoken with his mom. Fortunately for him, Shayla was one of those who believed in getting to church sometime between the greeting and the offering, and as long as she was there before the sermon she thought it was just fine. In a sense, a lot of people seemed to agree with her. Even though they did not go to church much, Hubert hated to be late. Hubert hated being late for anything. Hubert wanted to sit somewhere close to the front, so that he could be the one looking back at people, instead of people looking back at him. His mom was an usher at the church, so she was always early, and was the first person he saw when he stepped out of the truck.

"Hi, baby, I see you came out to get some of this good news," she said, coming over to give him a hug and a kiss on the cheeks.

"Yes, Ma, I needed a breath of fresh air, so I decided to come on out."

"Fresh air. Well, it cannot hurt any, with all of that mess you have going on in your life. You need more than a breath of fresh air, you need to realize what is really going on in your life, and that you are not as in charge as you think." She then gave him one of those *Son, you are in the right place* kind of hugs, and they walked in the church together. She looked like she still wanted to talk, but she knew that she had a job to do. So when they made it into the church, she clutched Hubert's hand real hard, and again kissed him on the cheek. She told him softly in his ear, "Whatever mistakes you make, I am always going to be your mom, and I am always going to love you."

For Hubert, that was a little unexpected, because even though he knew that he loved his mother, and that his mother loved him, it was something that they did not say it to each other that often. And this made him feel worse, because in his heart he knew that he had let her down.

So they started going through all of the church service rituals, the music, the greetings, the music, the church news, the music, the offering, and back to the music. Hubert would often look back to see if Shayla had walked in, just to see the look on her face, and try and figure what was going through her mind, or to see if she would even show up. And, right on her own schedule, she showed up between the music and the offering. She walked in by herself, and Hubert thought to himself, *Wow, she looks great as always.* One thing about her was that she hated for people to see her sweat, and, just looking at her, one would never believe that they had had the conversation they had last night. Hubert was in his own way happy to see that, but a little wary of her next move. She noticed him as soon as he noticed her. Shayla just stopped and stared at him, like they were playing the who-is-going-to-blink-first game. Hubert nodded his head to her; Shayla just rolled her eyes, and went and sat as far away from him as she could. She did, however, kiss his mother on the cheek as she seated her and gave her a church program. Hubert knew that he was waiting to see what she looked like, but it seemed as if everyone else was focused on the exact same thing. They would look at him, and then at her, then at him, and back at her—and this went on until it was time for the sermon.

Pastor Williams walked up—at this point everyone stood—and he opened his sermon with a prayer. With his hand at the end of the prayer, he signaled everyone to be seated.

"I want to talk to you today about"—he paused and wiped his mouth—"about bad decisions that lead to worse decisions. How many of you have made a bad decision and turn around and something else goes wrong because of that decision? Some of us experience that trickle-down effect, where every problem in our lives can somehow be related to that bad decision from the past."

He looked around at the audience, but, for some reason, it seemed to Hubert like he was talking directly to him alone. Hubert knew that he had felt this way before, but not this much. It felt to him like the beginning of a private session in the pastor's office.

Pastor Williams continued. "I want to use for a topic today 'You are the sum of your choices: Making the right decision first.' I will say it again for those who take notes, which should be everyone. People go to school and take notes, they start jobs and take notes, but come to church without a pen or a pad, many without even a Bible. But that is another message. Again for the note-takers, the topic is

'You are the sum of your choices: Making the right decision first.' Touch your neighbor and tell him, 'If you get it right the first time, you do not have to worry about it anymore.'" He smiled as the congregation did what he asked, and went on, "Touch your neighbor again, and tell him, 'Because I got it right the first time, I feel all right about it.' Today, we will be reading from Genesis chapter thirteen, and jumping around a little. Turn your Bibles with me, if you would, to Genesis chapter thirteen, verse nine, and we will read to…" He paused to think.

Now this was one of those churches where the deacon did the Scripture readings aloud, and the pastor elaborated on the verses.

Wiping his mouth again, the pastor continued. "Verses nine to eleven. Here, Abram—later called Abraham—and Lot, who was his nephew, were both rich in crops and cattle, and their herd men, or the people that work the crop and cattle, were having a big problem working together. Abram's solution to the problem was to separate. Read, deacon."

"'Is not the whole land before thee? Separate thyself, I pray thee, from me: if thou wilt take the left hand, then I will go to the right; or if thou depart to the right hand, then I will go to the left. And Lot lifted up his eyes, and beheld all the plain of Jordan, that it was well watered everywhere, before the Lord destroyed Sodom and Gomorrah, even as the garden of the Lord, like the land of Egypt, as thou comest unto Zoar. Then Lot chose him all the plain of Jordan; and Lot journeyed east: and they separated themselves the one from the other.'" The deacon finished the verse, and took a step back to wait until cued to read again.

"Thank you, Deacon," the pastor said, rubbing his hands together. "I want those of you that know the story of Sodom and Gomorrah—which is hopefully most of us? Amen. I want you to forget that you know that story, and work with me, and you will see where I am going with this. Lot, thinking that he was getting over on Abram, took what he thought was the more prosperous land, right?" Pastor Williams paused as the congregation nodded their heads, and then Pastor Williams continued his sermon.

"Sodom!" the pastor yelled loudly. "Sodom was a wicked place, where the Bible says the men sinned before God exceedingly, and guess what? This was Lot's new home, because, thinking he was getting over, he did not take into consideration what he was getting into. Touch your neighbor, and tell them, 'Before you think that you are getting over, you had better know what you are getting into.' Now, first of all, if you read verse fourteen, there was a war going on, and as you probably figured, Lot got caught up right in the middle. The kings of Sodom and Gomorrah fled, and they that remained fled to the mountains, the Bible said in verse ten. So who is left? Good ole Lot. So what happened? Read verses eleven and twelve, Deacon."

The deacon cleared his throat and began reading, "'And they took all of the goods of Sodom and Gomorrah, and all their victuals and went their way. And they took Lot, Abram's brother's son, who dwelt in Sodom, and his goods, and departed.'"

"Thanks, Deacon," Pastor Williams said, starting to walk around. "So Abram hears about this, and has to bring more than three hundred of his trained servants to help his brother's son. Who? Listen to this." He paused with one finger at his lips for the congregation to pay attention. He quietly said, "Thought that he was getting over. So Abram, like a good uncle, comes to Lot's rescue, and, with all of his people and goods, meets the king of Salem, Melchizedek, and then dips. Now while Abram is ready to get a name change plus blessings for generations to come, Lot on the other hand is still living in Sodom, and both Sodom and Gomorrah are getting worse in God's eyes. So let me tell you—I would let the deacon read it, but I have to let you guys get out of here today, and I do not want you to miss this. God tells Abraham—Abram's new name—'I am going to destroy Sodom and Gomorrah because their sin is very grievous,' meaning *very severe*. Get this, Abraham asks God, will he destroy the wicked with the righteous? If there are fifty righteous, will he spare the cities? And God replied yes. And Abraham goes on, and asks, if there be forty-five righteous, will he spare the cities? And God said yes, he would spare the city if there were forty-five righteous found. Abraham worked his way all the way down to ten people. So there were not even ten righteous people there. Now let me get back to the story, because I know that we have to go. God sent two angels to Sodom, and Lot saw them sitting at the gate, and went to meet them. He invited the angels to stay at his house, but before they could lay down and sleep, the men of this wicked city—the Bible says both young and old—were standing at the door, questioning Lot about the two men staying at his house, telling him, 'Bring them out so that we may get to know them.' Now do I have to tell you what they meant when they said 'that we may know them'? I will tell you this: Lot's response was that 'I would send out my two daughters that no man has known.' Now, think about this. All because he thought that he was getting over by getting the best land. Let me go on. So the angels had to eventually blind the men at the door, and told Lot to take his family in the morning to the mountains, for God is going to destroy this place. The next morning, Lot got his family up and headed for the mountains. The angels also told them—Deacon, I want you to read one more verse, and I promise you that we are getting ready to leave, but I just like the way you read. Genesis chapter nineteen verse seventeen."

The deacon smiled and the congregation laughed, and he began reading. "'And it came to pass, when they had brought them forth abroad that he said, "Escape for thy life, look not behind thee, neither stay thou in all the plain; escape to the mountain, lest thou be consumed.'"'"

"You put so much emphasis when you read, Deacon, thank you," the pastor said, and the congregation laughed again. "The angel specifically tells Lot, *look not behind thee*." Then the pastor yelled at the top of his lungs, "Don't look back! This is a simple instruction to follow, right? What happens, Lot's wife looks back, and turns into a pillar of salt. Now it is only Lot and his two daughters that survive this devastation. And get this, his oldest daughter tells the younger, 'Let us get our father drunk so that we may lay with him to preserve his seed,' and the older daughter does just that, and the next night the younger daughter does the same thing. These girls are getting their father drunk so that they can sleep with him!"

After ending this sentence, the pastor threw his handkerchief on the floor, looking mean in the face, then stood and stared at the congregation. He got himself together; an usher brought him another handkerchief. He wiped his face, and pointed at the congregation with the handkerchief, and continued. "What I am trying to get you to understand is that here is a man that had it all—herds of animals, tents, people working with him, and he was rolling with Abram. No worries, right? How many of you out there is or was experiencing this good life? But one bad decision changed everything. You thought it was going to get better, but it got worse and out of your control. Lot was kidnapped, offered his virgin daughters to sinners, his wife dies, and after that, his daughters get him drunk and slept with him." The pastor yelled again, "All because he wanted the better land, all because he wanted the better land. How many of you today made a bad decision, whether it was a sin or just to get the upper hand, and your plan backfired? How many of you married that man or that woman that so many people warned you about, and now your life is pure hell? How many of you took that first drink, that first inhale, that first needle, took that first item that did not belong to you, chased that first skirt or pretty boy, and now you can't stop? How many of you got that great deal on a house or a car that you knew you could not afford, took that job that you knew you were not qualified for, or simply ate that food you knew was not good for you?"

He looked at the congregation and calmly added, "I am going to say this last thing, then I am going to close. Every decision you make in life affects another decision, another situation, or another person. Make the right decision first. Think about who will benefit from your decision, think about who will get hurt from your decision. If you do anything, think about what is next before you have to make your decision. Before I have the altar call, I just want to say one thing, and I am closing for real this time. Just like Lot had Abraham interceding with God for him, we have Jesus Christ sitting at the right hand of God interceding for us. So even if you have made a bad decision, and even if things have gotten out of hand, remember that God loves you, and wants you to give your situation to him so that he can handle it. We cannot handle it ourselves, we are just going to make it worse. Make the right decision first."

Everyone stood and clapped as the ushers came down toward the front of the church. It was time for altar call. This was where the preacher asked if anyone wanted to accept Jesus Christ into their life. Pastor Williams continued on, "If there is anyone here that does not know Jesus as their personal savior, now is the chance. I am not asking you to stop everything that you are doing today, because if you could stop on your own, why would you need Jesus? Jesus said that he came to heal the sick. Jesus is that answer that will help you to start making better decisions, he is the only answer. Will there be anyone today? I will wait." No one came to the front of the church, and after a few minutes the pastor ended the service with a simple "God bless you, saints."

Everyone in the church who could stand was standing, clapping hands, and some crying. Others just looked around, praising or gazing. As for Hubert, he was in a completely confused state. His eyes were teary, his knees were shaking, and the thought going through his mind was whether this was God calling him. He had never felt this way before. Was that altar call for him? he thought. Should he have gone down? After hearing several messages all his life, he had never heard a sermon that touched him like this. As the people started walking out of the church, he just sat back in his seat as if to avoid the crowd, but, like many mothers, his mother knew that he was touched by the sermon.

"God was talking to you today, son," she said to him.

She reached out and gave him a big hug, and as he hugged his mother he noticed Shayla walking out of the church. She stopped and turned around, and for a moment everything seemed quiet, like they were the only two in the room. She looked at him for a few seconds, shook her head, and walked out of the church.

"That was your opportunity to give your life today, Hubert," his mother said as she let him go. "Come walk your mother to the car."

As Hubert walked with his mother, they were stopped by the pastor at the door.

"Sister Maggie Alexander, were you about to leave without speaking?" the pastor asked with a big smile on his face.

"I am sorry, Pastor, you seemed so busy, I did not want to bother you. But I tell you this, you preached a powerful word today. I think that you touched a lot of souls today," Hubert's mother said, looking a Hubert.

The pastor looked over at Hubert and reached out and shook his hand. "How has it been going, Brother Alexander?"

Now this was not that big of a town, and because Pastor Williams counseled and married Hubert and Shayla, the odds of him not knowing what had happened was slim, but it seemed as if he wanted Hubert to talk to him.

"Everything is going, Pastor."

"Going where, brother? I often hear people make that statement, 'everything is going.' Is everything going good, going bad, going crazy, or going completely out of control? Which one is it, son?" the pastor asked with Hubert's hand still in his. "Brother Alexander, if it is just going, we have to get control of it and make it go somewhere. And I recommend my driver Jesus Christ."

Hubert just shook his head in agreement. "Thank for the advice, sir. Come on, Mom, we have to go." They walked off to his mother's car, and he opened the door for his mother, kissed her on the cheek as she got in, and closed the door. She began to drive off, but then she suddenly stopped and backed up and rolled down the window. Hubert walked over to the car, thinking that something could be wrong, but his mother told him, "I love you, regardless of your mistakes. I love you, and God loves you too. Let him fix it." She then rolled the window up, and drove off.

Hubert walked back to his car with both hands on his head. This was a different day for him; everything seemed to be changing in his life, and this message seemed to sum up the changes. As he made it back to his truck, wondering where he would go next, he tried calling Shayla on the phone, but she did not answer. He then hung up, and called

Donovan, and what he told Donovan was much unexpected after the kind of events that had just taken place.

"Yo, Donovan."

"What's up, man?" Donovan answered.

"I need a drink, I will be over shortly."

"Wait, didn't you just leave church?"

"Yeah, I will tell you about it when I get there. Is Nikki there?"

"Yes, but they are getting ready to leave any moment now."

"All right, I will see you shortly."

Hubert made it to Donovan's, and Donovan was the only one home.

"Where are the girls?" Hubert asked.

"Nikki had some kind of practice. Cheerleading, band, basketball—she is into so much, and I cannot keep up. You look pretty sharp there, my friend. Coming from church?" Donovan asked.

"Yeah, man. It was wild, man. I think I actually felt something today. It was crazy," Hubert said as he walked in and sat on the couch.

"With that being said, buddy, you are going to pour your own trouble today. I am not playing with the man upstairs. I want to at least give you a couple of hours to marinate on your day and then I may pour you a hook. Right now, you still smell like the pews from the church, so you know where the glasses are and you know where everything is. Playa, you are on your own."

Hubert started fixing a drink, and asked the question. "So if someone comes into your club straight from a church function and orders a drink, you mean you do not give it to them?"

Without even thinking about the answer, Donovan responded, "Two things here to consider. One, this is my house and you are my friend. And two, they pay me to help them indulge, plus the bartender pours their drink. There is a difference."

Hubert, smiling, walking back to his seat with a drink, sarcastically added, "That is actually three things. What are you drinking anyway?"

"Vodka and orange juice, and I did not go to church today. Any more questions?"

"No, sir," answered Hubert, as he took a sip of his drink.

"So what was the sermon about anyway that got you running over hear like Ned the Wino?"

"It was just about choices we make in life, and the outcomes. It was deep, and I will leave it at that."

"On another subject, what are you going to do about a job, man? It is dog-eat-dog world out that joint, and everything is so job specific. It is truly an employer's market, so dress up that resume like you're taking it to church. There are just as many people looking for jobs as there are people looking for happiness."

"You are right. I think I will register on a few job sites and go and check a few local companies. I will find something. I am a pretty talented cat."

"You can always wait tables at the spot. I cannot offer that loaf of bread you were making, but I can probably give you that slice in the front and in the back." They both laughed, but Donovan, with a serious look suddenly on his face, continued. "No, give me a few weeks, and I may have a hustle for you, if things get shaky for you."

"Another one of your marketing strategies, Don?"

"When the time is right, I will let you know."

At that moment, Adrian and Nikki walked in. Nikki ran over and jumped on Hubert's lap. "Daddy, you should have seen me at practice. I don't think I missed one shot."

"Good job, baby. You are too big to be jumping on me like this. Now get your sweaty butt off my lap and go take a shower. You stink!"

"I do not," Nikki yelled, smelling her armpits.

"Hey, Hue," said Adrian. "You look nice today. You went to church?"

"Yeah, Hue," Donovan said, laughing. "Tell her how you were touched by an angel today."

"Shut up, man. Yes, I went to church and it was a good service."

"Good, you need to take your friend here," said Adrian as she popped Donovan upside the head.

"I am going when I am ready!" Donovan yelled.

"I just hope that you are ready before God requires your soul, baby," said Adrian. "Come on, Nikki, let's go upstairs so that Don and your dad can talk."

"She needs to go upstairs to take a shower," Hubert said, laughing.

"Dad, I do not smell. By the way, my first game is next Thursday at six thirty," she added as she walked up the stairs.

"I will be there, stinky. I love you."

"Hubert Alexander, we still need to talk when you get a chance," Adrian told him as she went up the stairs, pointing at him.

"Oh yeah," Donovan said. "How are things going with you and the wife?"

"It is what it is. I saw her today looking stressed, but still real cute so no one would notice. But I think that her primary focus was trying not to notice me. We stared at each other a few times, but she just seemed to not want to have any type of emotion toward me. But I can understand, man. I screwed this one up royally. I just have to figure out how I am going to fix it. I still have to talk to Adrian about child support payments, insurance, not to mention listen to her fuss. I have to try and mend things with Shayla somehow. I do love her, I just got caught up. Too many people do not realize how stupid it is until after they have already done it."

"Well, you got enough on your plate right now. You just worry about finding another job, about Shay, and your bills. I can handle Adrian and Nikki for now."

"No, I am going to still pay my support payments. It is just going to be coming from my severance and 401(k) if

I run out of money in the bank, until I get another job. I never wanted to use it, but a man's got to do what a man's got to do."

"If you don't mind me asking, how long can you last without working?" Donovan asked.

"I don't know. I will pay the truck off, and pay ahead on a few house notes. I don't know. Maybe six months, a year, year and a half," Hubert answered.

"Wow! That's great in this economy, pimp. But I told you, I got you later, trust me."

"Yeah, the problem is what happens with Shayla affects all of that. Not even thinking about the money, I don't want to lose her."

"You had better think about the money, and still make it work, Hue."

While the two sat talking, Hubert's cell phone went off. It was Eric.

"EP, what's the deal?"

"Yo man, it was some wild stuff already out there about you," said Eric in an excited voice.

"Calm down, E, what's up?"

"Peaches called and told C-Nice that you got fired on a fraternization charge for sleeping with Christina, and Monday she is going to be in charge. So you know that he is around here like it is Christmas just because she called him. She only did that because she wants the word to get out."

"Eric, I did not get fired. I am going to resign on Monday to prevent an uncontrollable chaos from occurring. With neither Chris nor myself there, the rumors will not last that long, hopefully."

"Hue, I still do not know what to say," said Eric. "I'm sorry, if there is anything I can do to help, let me know."

"Thanks, buddy, I'm going to be all right. True champions are built by overcoming their challenges. A boxer cannot place that champion belt around his waist if he has never fought anyone. I will get through this, my friend."

"All right man, I will talk to you later."

"I'll holler at you. Thanks for calling, E," Hubert said as he ended the phone conversation, and placed the phone back into its holder. He noticed that Donovan was staring at him strangely, and he looked back at him in the same manner. "What, man?"

"How is it that you have all of this positive, motivational advice for everyone, but your life choices are just out there," Donovan said, pointing to the left and the right. "You have given me so much advice since I met you, and I thank you. You just never listen when people tell you leave them tricks alone. You cannot always be the one talking but never listening."

"I know, man. I am a psychology major that does not work in his field, so I have to use it or lose it," Hubert answered, smiling.

Donovan snatched Hubert's empty glass, and walked toward the bar. "You don't need anything else to drink today, because that is the dumbest thing I ever heard you say!"

They both laughed, and at that moment, Adrian walked downstairs. "What are ya'll laughing about? I want to laugh."

"We are laughing at old Zig Ziglar the motivational speaker over here," Donovan answered.

"Who, Hubert?" Adrian asked.

"You know it," Donovan responded.

"Yeah, that's Hue. All his life, he wanted to give advice. Thinks he always knows something. His momma is the same way, so I guess it is hereditary. Hers is just on some deep religious tip. She makes you feel good by saying that whatever you are going through, she is going to find a spiritual silver lining. I remember when I told her that I was pregnant. She told me that everything was going to be all right, that she and God would be there with me. She said, just remember that I am not the first teenage pregnancy, and I will not be the last. She said I just needed to make a choice of what kind of mother I was going to be to my child." As Adrian was explaining an enormous smile appeared on her face, and she put one finger in the air and continued the story. "Then the bombshell. I told her that it was Hue's baby. At that point Mrs. Alexander looked like she needed strength from somewhere, and she looked at me and just stared, and there was a tear in the corner of her eye. I did not know if it was a tear of anger, joy, or what it was. I just stayed quiet. She looked at me, and tilted her head, and said, Hubert is the father? I said, Yes, ma'am, I have never been with no one else but him, and it was that one time. I was little frightened now. She just grabbed me real close and held me and said, God got it, baby, God got it. She held me real close for about a minute, squeezing me actually. When she let me go, I was able to exhale." Hubert, Donovan and Adrian laughed as she continued. "No, seriously, but when she walked away, she turned and looked back at me, and told me in that voice that draws everyone in, I love you, baby. Aww, that made me feel so good, relaxed, and loved, and now ya'll don't get me all emotional. I am going back upstairs."

Adrian then turned and walked up the stairs, and by time she reached the top stair, Donovan called for her. "Adrian."

"Yes, baby?"

Donovan turned around and stood up where she could see him, and opened his arms to her, smiling, and softly said, "I love you, baby." He and Hubert both laughed.

"I love you too, silly," she responded as she went into the room.

Donovan looked up the stairs to see if Adrian had gone into the bedroom, and came back and asked Hubert, "So you mean you guys only did it once?"

"What are you talking about?" Hubert asked, puzzled.

"When Adrian was telling the story, she said that she told your mother that you guys only did it once, and that it was her first time."

"Man, what made you ask that?" Hubert asked.

"Just wondering, man, just wondering," Donovan replied, looking serious.

"Man, are you serious?"

Donovan did not say a word, but only looked at the bedroom and back at Hubert, waiting for his response.

"Man, yes, we done it more. We were young. She lived right beside me, and after her father died, she was always over our house. After the Nikki was born, we still had time alone because my mom was always gone. So, yes, there were more times," Hubert explained.

"Well, thanks for being honest, I just wanted to know."

"No problem. Are you drunk?"

"Not yet, I have to go to work tonight for a while."

There seemed to be a little tension for a while with no talking. The two just drank and listened to the music. Then Nikki came running down the stairs.

"I am out of the sweaty clothes now, but I did not stink because I never stink," Nikki said.

"Baby, after helping raise you for almost eleven years," Hubert responded, "there were some early days when you smelled awful. I would put the diaper in a plastic bag, put the plastic bag in the trash, put the trash in the dumpster, and call the people and pay them extra to come and empty the dumpster."

Hubert laughed as Nikki punched him in the arm. Donovan only had a small smile on his face.

"Stop talking about my baby," Adrian said as she walked down the stairs.

"You know that I am telling truth. I use to think you were putting cheap wine in the bottles," Hubert added, still laughing.

"But that is different, Daddy. Every baby's diaper smelled," Nikki said, pointing at Hubert.

"You are right, baby, you did not smell any different. I told you leave my baby alone," Adrian said defending her baby. But then she saw at the grim look on Donovan's face. She walked over to Donovan and kissed him on the lips. "What's wrong with my big baby?" she asked, referring to Donovan.

Donovan just looked at her and smiled. Adrian then looked at Hubert for a response, but Hubert just shrugged his shoulders.

"Donovan's good, but I am about to get up out of here. Bye, stinky," Hubert said as he grabbed Nikki and squeezed her really tight. "Thanks for the drinks, Donovan. Bye, family." He gave Donovan a hug and pound and headed for the door.

"Hue, don't forget we still need to talk," Adrian said.

"We will. But, look, I need a favor from you," Hubert said then looked over at Donovan. "No, I need a favor from the both of you. I need you guys to really talk to my girl for me."

"When are we going to talk?" Adrian asked.

"After the game next Thursday," Hubert replied, looking down at Nikki. "You thought I had forgotten, didn't you?"

Nikki just smiled as Hubert headed for the door, but before he left, Nikki yelled out, "Bye, Daddy, tell Mrs. Shay I said hey!"

"I will, baby, you guys take it easy," Hubert said as he walked out the door.

8

A Change in Lifestyle

It was Monday morning; the weekend was over. Hubert awoke still in the motel room, and sat up in bed. He looked at himself in the mirror and took a deep breath, and then exhaled. Hubert then remembered that he was supposed to have his letter of resignation for Mr. Marshall ready by morning. He called down to the front desk for access to a computer, but the receptionist informed him that the computer room was closed down for repairs and upgrades. Hubert had forgotten to pack his laptop, and he did not want to type the letter at the office. So he decided to go to his house, type the letter from home, and take it to the job. On his way to the house, he figured he would call Shayla just to let her know that he had to come by. The phone rang the first time with no answer. So Hubert was thinking that she was either in the shower or she still did not want to talk. Hubert thought that, whatever the case, he still needed to get into his house and get to the laptop, so he called once again.

"Hello," Shayla answered.

"Good morning," Hubert said, his eyes opening wide in his surprised that she answered.

"Good morning, can I help you?"

"I have to come over there and get my laptop."

"That's fine, I will be gone by time you get here," Shayla replied quickly.

"So you are determined not to see me?" Hubert asked.

"Hue, what do you want me to say? Let's just kiss and make up? You want me to say I understand why you did this to our family? You want me to say I forgive you, come home? Because if that is what you are thinking, if that is what you want, you will be waiting a lifetime," Shayla said with finality.

Just then, the door opened, and Hubert was already in the house before Shayla could leave. He walked up the stairs to the bedroom, where Shayla had been doing her hair at the mirror before Hubert had called. They both just stared at one another. Shayla still had the phone in her hand.

"Hey," Hubert said, like he was lost for words.

"Please get your laptop and leave," Shayla said very calmly.

"I am sorry, baby," Hubert replied.

This time Shayla was a little more firm. "Hue, please get your laptop and get out! It is in the spare bedroom on the bed, with a lot of other mess from your job."

Hubert was a little confused as to why the laptop or other papers from the job would be in the spare bedroom, when he had an office in the house. He did not even bother to ask. When he got into the room, papers were scattered across the bed, like someone had been looking for something. Hubert knew then that Shayla had been through his things. Still, no question. Hubert grabbed his laptop, went downstairs to his office, and began to type his resignation letter. As he was typing, he looked back over his shoulder, toward the door, and Shayla was standing there watching him. He did not know how long she had been standing there, or why.

Again, the two just stared at one another. Then suddenly Shayla asked, "What are you typing, anyway? If I may ask?"

"Marshall said that I have to turn in my resignation letter by this morning," Hubert responded, sounding sad.

"So she worked with you?" Shayla questioned.

Hubert still typed, acting as if he did not hear her question.

"I guess you really messed this one up." Shayla then looked down at her watch. "So you are actually going in late, to get fired. What are you going to do about a job?" Shayla asked.

Hubert stopped typing and looked up at Shayla, and then started rubbing his face like he was looking for sympathy. He then shook his head, indicating that he did not have an answer.

"Well, I am going to my job. Lock up before you leave. And Hue," Shayla said with an extremely serious expression on her face, "Take everything that you are going to need. I do not want any more surprise visits today." She then walked out of the house. Hubert called her name several times, but to no avail.

Hubert finished the resignation letter and headed to J. Marshall Marketing for the very last day as an employee. As he sat in the car, Hubert contemplated how he wanted to deal with the people on the job. What he would say, how he would act, and how he would leave. His entrance strategy was just as important as his exit strategy. Hubert knew that all eyes would be on him as he walked into that building for the last time, being one of the head executives there. This was a firm where rumors were sometimes just as important as accounts to some of the workers. Hubert tried to process all of this information before he finally decided to walk in. As he walked into the building, the halls were clear. This meant that there must have been a firm-wide meeting at that time. So Hubert walked into his office, placed the resignation letter in a manila envelope, and sat it on his desk. He then proceeded to clean out his desk. As Hubert was cleaning, he heard taps at the door. He looked up, and it was Alisha with no real expression on her face.

"Can I come in?" she asked.

Hubert never responded, just continued to pack his thing up, but still Alisha walked in and stood at the desk.

"Look," she started to explain. "This is not how I wanted to be promoted. I wanted your job because I think that I am better than you at doing it. I wanted to continue to challenge you on acquisitions of new business and contracts. You made me better, you made me think outside the box at times. I don't want the job because you are leaving, I wanted to take it from you, Alexander," Alisha said, smiling. "When you were at the top, I could talk about you. Now that I am going to be at the top, who will I talk about?"

"Peaches, you will always find someone to talk about. But you will be too busy to talk about anything for the next few months. I can promise you that," Hubert added, pointing at his in-box.

"I will be all right. Marshall is going to send out a memo this morning stating that were are going through a transition period right now."

Shaking his, head Hubert responded, "Good idea. As long as you do not push back too many deadlines."

"Yeah, you're right. Marshall also said that even though he thinks the customer is always right, the employees are not machines. He said he does not want to lose any business, but he also does not want to overwork the team," Alisha said.

"Makes sense," Hubert replied. "How is he anyway?"

"It is a rough and tough Monday for everyone, Alexander. This entire situation is just awful, but it is what it is. And, Alexander, on that note, I was also sent here to retrieve your resignation letter," Alisha added with a sorrowful look on her face.

Hubert just looked down at the desk where his letter was. Alisha reached down and picked up the letter and headed out, but before she left she turned and said, "I heard Copeland needs a media director and a graphics assistant. I'm just saying."

Hubert reached inside one of the boxes and pulled out a pack of orange Tic Tacs and tossed them to Alisha. "Peaches, I enjoyed working with you. I am sorry that it had to end this way. But for the records, you will never be better than me at this."

"We will never know now. So who will bring me Tic Tacs?"

"Your boy C-Nice, I guess," Hubert responded, laughing.

"He did ask me one time why was I sleeping with you for candy when he offered to put rims on my car and can get nothing from me," Alisha said, laughing.

"So many people think we crossed that line," Hubert expressed.

"Alexander, that is because you have crossed that line with so many people," Alisha stated, smiling as she walked back in. "I don't deny or confirm. It is not their business. Give me a hug so I can go and get back to work." The two shared a close, long hug, and when they were finally finished, Alisha pulled back and just smiled, pointing the hand with the candy at Hubert. "You are bad. Behave, but take care of yourself, Alexander."

"I will," Hubert said as Alisha walked out the door.

Hubert continued packing with the smile still on his face, when he heard Clayton's voice.

"I want to smile too. Tell me what's so funny?"

"What do you want Clayton?" Hubert asked.

"I'm just checking on you. I come in here and see you smiling on your last day. Ain't no way I would be smiling. I would be fighting for my job. Lose my job behind some trick, I wish."

"Clayton, let me tell you, that is the difference between you and I. So if you do not need anything, let me finish what I am doing."

"All right, man, I will leave you alone. Let me go and see if Peaches needs any help. I heard she was short a person too," Clayton added, rubbing his hands together before he finally walked out.

Others would come in and bid Hubert farewell or just wish him the best at whatever he would do. Hubert made many trips out to his truck, taking pictures, flowers, clocks, and many different items. On his last trip from the office, Hubert looked around one last time to make sure that he was not forgetting anything. Then he just stopped and thought about what was really going on. He was leaving a company that he helped to prosper. A company where he had started from the mailroom and, in a matter of years, moved his way to the top. He had trained so many employees. He was responsible for acquiring so many of the company's accounts. This was his house, but when Hubert walked out this time, he would have to surrender his key. Hubert finished looking around the room; he concluded that it was not time for him to leave. As he turned to walk out of the office, there was Mr. Marshall standing in the door.

"So you were going to leave and not say good-bye, Alexander?" Mr. Marshall asked.

"Sir, I figured being you had Peaches to pick up the resignation letter, you really did not want to see me," Hubert replied.

"She asked whether she could pick it up, to learn the cancellation process for when an associate quits. I was not even thinking it. I guess she threw that in your face."

"No, sir. Actually, she was gracefully sincere. I do not know what she is saying now, but earlier she seemed somewhat concerned," Hubert explained.

Mr. Marshall smiled and reached out his hand to shake Hubert's "This is a sad day for this company. I cannot express gratitude for all that you'd done. I wish that there was another way. If you need anything, a reference, a letter of recommendation, or even money, you have my number. I know that I was upset on the phone, but it is with my deepest regrets that I have to do this. I can continue to pay you for the next three months and you can keep all of your benefits until then. After that, you are on your own, son."

With hands still together, Hubert looked at Mr. Marshall with an exceedingly sorrowful look on his face, and began to speak. "Mr. Marshall, I am so sorry for the mess that

I have made. I am also sorry for the position that I have placed you and your company in. You are a people's leader and I know that J. Marshall will survive and maintain its success. I have learned so much from you over the years. I appreciate every opportunity that you have given me, and I will never forget all you have done. Again, I am sorry that I let you down." Before the moment could get too emotional, Hubert hugged Mr. Marshall and grabbed the last small box. "I guess this is it, sir."

"I guess it is. And, son, you did not let me down, you let yourself down. Now you have to go through the process of building yourself back up. I know that you have a lot of supporters out there that are pulling for you. Alexander, my best advice for you is to use wisdom in every decision you make in order to get your life back. Yes, J. Marshall will be fine, but you have become an island that is going to need a lot of resources to get you back on your feet. Choose those resources very wisely, or you will find yourself being that deserted island that no one wants to visit."

The two shook hands one more time, and walked out together before taking separate ways. Hubert was surprised that he had made his departure with not much drama. He walked out to his truck, looked back at the building one more time, smiled, and drove off. As he was driving, he could feel his cell phone vibrating. He looked at the phone and it was Shayla. Hubert quickly answered. "Hello."

"Hello, Hue, how are you?" Shayla asked, sounding concerned, which seemed odd to Hubert considering her actions earlier.

"I'm good, as to be expected with everything going on. Thanks for asking," Hubert replied.

"So what are you going to do about a job?" Shayla asked.

"I heard that Copeland Marketing had some opening, and if I can get my foot in the door, I can work my way up."

"I hope that it works out for you, Hubert."

"I hope that I can work it out for us, baby," Hubert said in desperation. Things were quiet on the phone for a few seconds when Shayla began to speak again.

"Hue, the reason that I am calling, it's because I put in for some time off. I am moving back home with my mom and dad for a while. I took a month off, and I told the school that I would let them know if I would be returning. I need to get away. I need to think. So I wanted you to know that you do not have to stay at the hotel anymore. I am leaving this evening."

"Shayla, please do not leave me now," Hubert begged with even more desperation. "I need you. I know that I messed up, but I need you around so that we can work through this. Stay in the house, I will move in with my mom. Just do not leave."

"Hubert, understand this," Shayla explained in a totally different tone. "I am calling to let you know, I did not have to call. We share a house, but I do not want to share anything else with you right now. I detest you as a man, let alone a husband," she said slowly. "You chose this. I am calling your mother and letting her know. And, Hubert I do not know when you will be hearing from me again. Bye!" Shayla then turned the phone off before Hubert could even respond.

Hubert just shook his head, thinking to himself, *I did not expect that.* He went back to the hotel to pick up his clothes. It was getting close to twelve, which was the checkout time. Since he now knew that he would not be spending another night, he had to get his things out. If he or his things were still in the room after twelve, the hotel would charge him for another night. After gathering all of his clothes, Hubert went on his laptop and retrieved the information for Copeland Marketing. He gave them a call, and they set up an interview for him the following week. He also checked some other sites, just to see what else was out there. While working on the computer, Hubert's phone went off again. This time it was Eric.

"Yo," Hubert answered.

"What's up man, I did not see you at work today. What time did you get there?"

"Oh, E, my bad, it was early. When you guys were having your meeting. I was cleaning out my desk. I didn't want to make too much of a scene. So I figured I would dip in and dip out."

"I thought that more talk was going to fly, but actually more people were in shock that you left. Marshall said that you chose another path, so we had to pick up the pieces and step it up for a while. It was a pretty good speech. Peaches spoke about her expectations, but nothing is really going to change much, I hope. So people think that you are starting your own firm. And just to let you know, I would work for you."

"Thanks, man, I know," Hubert responded. "I do not really know what is next, but I just have to start from somewhere."

"Look, Peaches did tell C-Nice that she told you of a few places hiring. I would not trust her with any recommendations, Hue."

"Shayla told me that she was leaving today. I'm good for a while financially, but right now, E, I have to take what I can get. Things may get a little tight, and I want to be on top of them before they fall apart. So I am going to try Peaches's lead," Hubert explained.

"I understand. And sorry to hear about Shay, boss. What are you guys going to do?" Eric asked.

"E, I want my marriage back. I will live separated. I will go through counseling. I will do what it takes to get my wife back."

"Did you tell her that?"

"Man, whenever I start talking about us, she flips. I am hoping that time will heal this wound, and we can get on with our lives."

"So are you going to make it to the round table this evening?" Eric asked.

"What time?"

"I guess about five forty-five."

"Is your boy coming?"

"Unfortunately."

"Well, I am not doing anything anyway. I will run by the house for a while, and I will be there by time you guys get there," Hubert said. Then there was a knock at the door; it was housekeeping. "Let me get up out of here before I get charged for another night. I will see you there, E."

So Hubert left the hotel, and dropped his clothes off at the house.

Later that evening, Hubert was the first of the round table crew to make it to DA's. He saw Donovan in the back office at his desk, and walked right in.

"I used to have a desk until this morning," Hubert said sarcastically. Donovan looked up, smiled, and came over and gave Hubert the usual hug and pound.

"My man, what's the deal? EP said you were coming to join us at the round table today." Donovan looked down at his watch. "Well, we still have time. Grab yourself something to eat. Let me finish up some business, and I will be out by time the others get here." Donovan went back to his desk, and continued to work.

Hubert went out and sat in the bar area and waited to be served. The others would gradually show up until eventually everyone was there. Everyone spoke and took their seats at the table.

"What's up, every one?" Donovan said. "It seems like we have everyone from the last round table. Even Robert from the IRS. What's up, Bobby?" Everyone laughed while Robert nodded his head. Donovan called over a waitress, and placed the order for drinks. Then he asked, "Okay, who's up first?"

"I will go first," said Victor. "I want to know what really happened with customer service. True, there are a few of people out there who care and take pride in whatever service they provide, but overall, customer service sucks. People do not pay attention to what they are doing. No one has a personality, and they get so offended with the simplest complaint."

Clayton jumped in laughing. "Are you sure you are not just pissing them off, and are mad because they are mad?"

"No, if I place an order for a service then it is your job to provide that service for me. I should get the best service that my money is paying for. Regardless of how your day is going," Victor quickly interjected.

"Can I take this one, being an owner and manager, and I am sure that Hue would agree?" Donovan started.

Before he could finish talking, Clayton took his elbow and nudged Eric and said, "You may be a manager, but Alexander is not."

The table got really quiet, when Robert from the IRS looked over at Hubert and asked, "You are not a manager anymore?"

"Let us get back to where we were, please, before we were rudely interrupted," Donovan said, looking over at Clayton. "From a manager's standpoint, your leader should fall in direct responsibility. Everyone has a bad day, but each employee should be an exact reflection of the company. With the appropriate training, and making sure that everyone is doing the jobs the standard way, you eliminate confusion. If you are rendering a service, you have to have extensive training on almost every situation, along with the basic training in what is expected of the employee. So many people this day in time are only working for the paycheck. A great leader is one that can search this person out, and replace him with someone who cares. The most important fact is that the leader has to care. Even if you are not paying your workers enough money, you should always treat them like they are worth so much more."

"If I may jump in," Hubert said. "Donovan is a hundred percent right. I too have had experience bad customer service on far too many occasions. Attitude is half the battle, plus being able to feel like part of that vision that you are working for. If you are selling fries, tires, or insurance, you should make me feel like I am getting the best the company has to offer. All of that starts with proper training and leadership. And because so many of the low-paying jobs out there have such a big turnover rate, employers do not take the appropriate time to train the worker. Many of them don't even really screen their workers, unless it is that drug screen. So again I would agree with Donovan that it is all about ownership, leadership, and realizing that every employee clocked in is a reflection of the company."

"Anyone else?" Donovan asked. Robert raised his hand to speak, and everyone at the table laughed. "Go ahead, Robert."

"I don't have anything to say, but I wanted to say that you guys are pretty good. You should come to DC and speak to the IRS. It made a lot of sense."

"Well, thank you for that compliment. It does seem like the IRS had to go to a 'Be a Jerk' boot camp before they started working. But it would work for them also. Who's next, and does anyone want a bottle of wine?" Donovan asked.

"No, I am good with the beer," Hubert replied.

"Naw, I am straight, thanks," Eric responded.

"Keep the beer coming, this is getting good," Robert added.

"I'm with Bobby. Keep the brews coming," Clayton said, laughing.

"Yeah, the beer is fine," Victor responded as they all looked down at Latrell, who did not drink beer or any alcohol for that matter.

"You know what," Latrell said with an enormous smile on his face. "I would like a glass of wine."

Everyone looked at him again, surprised. Donovan quickly called the waitress over to get him a glass of wine.

Clayton, looked down the table at Latrell and said, "I know that Jesus Junior is not taking a drink."

Latrell looked down at Clayton, and quickly responded, "I asked for a drink, not to get drunk. The Bible never condemned drinking wine but getting drunk. It actually said that even a deacon of the church could drink some wine, but not much. Anything in excess can be considered a sin, from drinking to eating. In the end, God is not upset at what you do to yourself, but you also cannot be mad at God for what excessive indulgences do to you. Your family, your life, and your health can all be affected by those indulgences. Cancer, cirrhosis of the liver, STDs, and many other diseases can be limited if we focus on how we live our lives. Drinking too much, smoking too much, eating too much, and I will not get into the indulgence of our sexual appetite. They all can have a disastrous effect on our future. That is why God does not want you to do them. And with that being said, I am going to drink this one glass of wine, and enjoy it."

"Hear, hear," Donovan said as he held up his glass to toast Latrell's comments. "Well said, Pastor Latrell. You slipped a good conversation in and didn't even know it. Does anyone want to respond on what Victor just preached—I mean said?"

"So you mean that you can still go to church after drinking or smoking or running women?" Victor asked curiously.

"Alexander did it," Clayton said, laughing.

No one really thought that Clayton's comments were that funny, but Donovan did smile and look over at Hubert, who acted as if he hadn't even heard what was said.

Latrell went on to explain. "Good question. No, God does not want you to continuously go to the church knowing that you are sinning still. It is a process, Vic. I was always told that you have to get the fish out of the water first before you can clean it. So God knows your heart better than you do. Just like that fish, getting you out of the water is like getting you out of the world. And once you accept Jesus, the cleansing process starts. God gives you a clean heart, but you still have to go through the process of getting the world out of you. And that process will last until someone places you in a box. You have to fight the world's temptations every day. Jesus is there to guide you only if you let him."

The table got very quiet, and every one took a drink, and seemed to be meditating on Latrell's speech. No one said a word, until Donovan looked around the table and spoke out. "So I guess all of you going to church Sunday."

Everyone laughed, but they could tell that Latrell had changed the atmosphere and the mode of the conversation.

"I will go next," Robert called out to get things going again.

"You going to church, or you got a topic?" Donovan asked and everyone laughed.

"No, I have a topic. Why do you guys think that there are so many violent crimes being committed by so many young people these days?" Robert asked.

Hubert, who had been reserved for a while, responded. "I think that there are several reasons, but most of them go back to upbringing. How you were raised affects a lot of the choices that you make. What you seen and what you heard has more bearing than what you were taught. You cannot discipline your kids the same way, the schools cannot discipline your kids the same way. Times are different now. Some children would rather talk to a shrink now than talk to their parents. Other kids are just raising themselves, thinking no one cares."

Clayton jumped in talking loud, trying hard to prove a point. "That's the problem right there! Yeah, times are different, and I get that. What you need is some of the mothers back in them homes raising those kids. The only thing that is growing faster than daycares are veterinarian hospitals, but that is a whole new topic in itself! I have nothing against a woman working, but who is really raising the kids, who is really nurturing now with the mother and the father at work? The television, the video games, the radio, and their peers are raising these kids. Most of the parents are just providing for the children. I was at the gas station a few days ago, and a woman stopped in, driving one of those eighteen-wheel trucks, talking about how they had to get back to Texas to get to those bad kids of hers. We are so focused on the money that we lose focus of the family."

"So you do not think that the woman needs to work?" Hubert asked Clayton.

"No, that is not my issue. My issue is knowing your role as a parent," Clayton said defending his stance.

"Even though times have changed, Clayton does have a point," Latrell spoke out. "Not that I have a problem with the woman working, but I do agree that it does play a part. Unfortunately, we created this beast. The woman was once the parent that provided most of the nurturing, prepared the meals, helped with homework, and took care of the home. Society is totally different now, and I think for two reasons. One, the change in economics. A one-income household struggles to survive and is forced to live from paycheck to paycheck depending on his job. We have created the two-story-house-with-a-garage image, and everyone is forced to keep up. So now we're not only both working, but we are working around the clock, we are bringing work home, and I can see us losing focus on the family, because we are too busy keeping up with the Joneses. And two, and probably most important, is part of the topic we talked about earlier. Because of the lack of commitment, the lack of self-discipline, and simply the lack of control, we have so many single mothers out there that have to work. I do not have a wife yet, because I know that God has someone specifically for me, and I have to wait for her. Yes, I will date, but that is as far as it will go. You have boys and girls fifteen and sixteen years old, sometimes younger, who are out here having sex. Can you imagine how many partners most people will have if they start having sex at fifteen? So along with sex come the consequences. Now we have all of these irresponsible, immature mothers with irresponsible, immature daddies. But wait, there is more, like the commercial says. She gets with someone else, he gets with someone else, and they have more kids eventually. So now we have all these children with different parents. It is great if the father stays in the child's life, but in far too many instances that is not the case. So the mother has to work, go to school for a better job, or get on the system. Imagine this being a problem throughout our entire American society. America tells adults that you have to work to survive, and America tells our children on national television that you have to be in a relationship. America has so many crime shows on national television where you can see a dead body every night of the week. America creates video games where the object is to kill, with the graphics becoming more realistic every day. America promotes music with so much sexual and violent tension that I am amazed that we are not seeing more violence. So to answer the question, it goes back to being a responsible, mature parent even before the baby enters the womb. Parents really have to focus on balance, and time management. They have to take a parental role in their child's life, or, like many situations, society will. As for America, the leaders of our nation really need to sit down to evaluate and consider if they need to be more responsible about what we call entertainment."

"Brother, you need to drink wine at every round table. That was good. Just make sure that you have some men around you. Some woman might take offense to the old-school image of the woman at home cooking and cleaning," Hubert explained.

"Alexander, it worked for centuries," Latrell replied.

"I know, man, you made a lot of good points. Just remember what I told you. Times are different now. What was wrong yesterday may be right tomorrow," Hubert added.

"Just because the majority agrees that it is right does not make it right," Latrell answered.

"Good point, but on another note. You mean you have never been with a woman?" Hubert asked as everyone looked at Latrell for his answer.

Latrell paused for a moment, and looked down at his watch. "My, it is time for me to go. All right, fellows, great round table. I am out!"

Donovan, laughing as Latrell was getting himself together to leave, added, "Yeah, guys, it was a good talk. I am going to head back in there and do some work. The drinks are on the house, stay as long as you want. Well, let me correct that, one more pitcher is on the house."

"I'm good too. I'm going to get ready and head out. Do not give Latrell anymore wine. I have never heard him talk so much," Hubert added after Donovan had gone.

"Where are you headed?" Eric asked Hubert.

"I'm going to run by the house and play with this resume site."

Hubert got up and left the table, stopping by to let Donovan know he was heading out. As he was driving up to the house, he saw Shayla walking out of the house and to her car. He parked his truck behind her so that she would be blocked in. She placed a box on top of her car and walked back to Hubert's driver-side window. Hubert let the window down.

"Please move your truck, Hue."

"Please talk to me."

"I have nothing to say to you."

"Please say something, just have a simple conversation with me for a minute, and I promise I will move the car," Hubert pleaded.

"So did you call Copeland?"

"Yes, and I have an interview next week."

"Is that the only place you checked?"

"Yes, Marshall is paying me for a few months, so I need a job, but I am not desperate yet. I will probably get the job at Copeland. I will be back on my feet before you know it," Hubert said confidently.

"Well, your minute is up, I have to go."

"Do you still love me?"

"Move the truck, Hue, we are not having this conversation," Shayla firmly answered.

"Shay, tell me, please. I want to know if I still have a chance."

"You said one minute, and you promised that you would move out of my way. You can't seem to commit to any other promises you made me, how about you start by committing to that one."

Hubert just looked at Shayla and smiled and put his truck in reverse and backed out, and pulled up beside her car. He got up out of the truck as she was getting into her car. He walked over and stood at her window, hoping that she would let it down. Shayla knew that Hubert was standing at the window, but ignored him. She actually made a phone call. Hubert stood at her window until she finished her conversation. She finally decided to let the window down.

"What do you want now, Hue," Shayla asked sounding annoyed.

"Just to let you know, I love you. I know that I made mistakes, but I am never going to stop loving you."

"Did you take a picture from the wall downstairs?"

"Yes," Hubert answered.

The two stared at each other and no one said a word. Finally, Shayla nodded her head as if to say okay. She then put the window up, and backed out and left.

Days went by, and Hubert and Shayla had innumerable small talks on the phone but nothing groundbreaking.

Whenever Hubert would say something about them trying to work on the relationship Shayla would end the conversation. So his personal life was still rocky and now it was time for the first interview. Hubert got himself together and was prepared for the big day.

Copeland was a close competitor with J. Marshall Marketing. Hubert had actually applied there as soon as he graduated from college, but to no avail. Back then they wanted more experience, when he was looking for an entry-level position.

So here Hubert was, sitting at a table across from four faces deep into his resume, with questions coming from every end. Hubert, who was very sharp and known for giving his all in everything he did, had no problem answering the questions. That is, until…

"Mr. Alexander," said one of the female interviewers.

"Yes, ma'am," Hubert answered confidently.

She continued smiling. "I am very impressed with your resume, your drive, and your attitude."

Hubert, who was also smiling, sat back in his chair nodding his head, but knowing that she was not finished.

"But, Mr. Alexander, one has to wonder what makes a man holding your executive position job at Marshall just up and leave a job after all of these years. Based on your application and resume, you did a lot for this company and they were compensating you very well, even better than we are actually willing to offer you."

As she made that statement, she looked around at the others as if she wanted some support from them. The other three calmly stared at Hubert in anticipation of a response.

Through the entire quest for another job, this was the first time that this question had arisen. Hubert was obviously not going to tell the truth, because the interview seemed to be going so well. He did not want to jeopardize his chances, so he did what he thought would work: he lied.

"Well, ma'am," clearing his throat. "You get to the point sometimes in your life where you feel that a change is necessary. And," he added, putting his hand on his chest, "deep in your heart, if you know that change is needed, you cannot just base your decisions on money or a position if you are just not happy." Hoping they bought it, he ended there.

Again, this same interviewer continued to question. "I just don't understand, and I am curious as to why you did not seek a new job first, and then place a two weeks' notice." She looked down at the paperwork. "You did put in a two weeks' notice or letter of resignation in, right?" She again looked at the other interviews with doubts about his answer.

Before Hubert could even answer, one of the other interviewers added, "I think what she is asking is what is it about a job of your capacity and pay in this economy that could make you just up and quit without any other options. Do you understand what I am saying?"

The room went quiet and again all eyes were on Hubert for a response. Hubert, now seeming a little agitated, nodded his head, confirming that he understood the line of questioning. He looked over at the female interviewer who started the whole interrogation process and began to speak. "Have you ever heard of an uncontrollable chaos?"

They all looked at him and at each other, hoping that this was a rhetorical question.

Hubert continued. "Sometimes you give a company all you have, but still you are not happy, you are just doing your job. This can have a negative effect on your personal life, your marriage or relationship, parenting, and the type of person that you may become outside of work. And, ma'am"—looking at the interviewer—"there is a limit that some people can be pushed to, and I felt that I had reached mine. And to save my family, my health, and my dignity, I walked."

Hubert looked around at the interviewers as he sighed and leaned back in his seat, hoping to win some compassion or sympathy.

Unfortunately the response was just the opposite. "That was very inspirational, Mr. Alexander, but I still do not get it," that same curious female interviewer said, shaking her head. "Mr. Alexander, what happens if you are hired here and you and the company are doing well, but again you somehow reach one of these"—expressing with the two quotation fingers in the air—"'uncontrollable chaotic' moments in your life? Do you then give up, and leave us also? You were one of Marshall's top executives, so you know the risk of doing this. This business is about assets and liabilities. Right now, if you were in our shoes, which one of these characteristics do you honestly think you portray?"

"Ma'am," Hubert said clearing his throat. "I just need a chance to get my feet wet. I have a lot of great ideas and I could surely bring value to your already distinguished comp—"

Before Hubert could even finish getting the word *company* out of his mouth, the interviewer blurted out, "I still don't get it!"

Now Hubert's agitation started turning into frustration and he let it get the best of him shouting out, "Well, with all due respect, ma'am, maybe it is not for you to get!" He then put his hands in the air, shaking his head from side to side, calming himself down. "Look, I know I can bring a lot to the table, but maybe it is both of our loss today." He then picked up all of his things and looked over at the female interviewer giving him all the trouble, shaking his head. "You guys have a great day, and I hope that you find what you are looking for."

As he walked out, they all look at each other with an indescribable look on their faces, wondering what had just happened. When Hubert was out of the room, one of the male interviewers looked over at the female interviewer and asked, "Do you know him?"

And she quickly responded, "No, but I know his kind, and something is not right."

All of the other interviewers stared at her.

"What?" she asked.

One of the interviewers added, "I hope that you are right."

As for Hubert, he walked out in disbelief. He just sat in his truck rubbing the top of his head wondering what he was going to do. The normal response was always to go and see Donovan at the restaurant.

On his way there, his mother called. "Hello," Hubert said, fixing the Bluetooth earpiece in his ear.

"Hey, Hue, I was just calling to check up on you. So how is the job hunt coming along?"

"It's not."

"Didn't you have an interview today?"

"Yeah, how did you know?"

"I talked to Shayla a few days ago. Speaking of her, Hue, what are you guys going to do?"

"Mom, you have to ask her, but I know that she is going to tell you that she wants nothing to do with me."

"I know, baby, but both of you need to take it to God."

"We can take it anywhere you want to take it, but she hates me, and right now there is nothing that I can do to change that."

"Hubert, that girl don't hate you. But you do need to give your life to Christ, and let him slowly work on you. Maybe in time, by chance, she will see the change in you over time and will at least consider listening to your side. And one day maybe she'll even consider reconciling what God already put together. You young kids get married these days not realizing that this thing is more than a relationship, it is a covenant before God, with tough rules that require tough love and two responsible adults. The problem today is that too many irresponsible kids calling themselves adults are getting married. Then when things get tough, they want out. Everything is so easy to get out of these days. Lord, help them! You get a good lawyer or a good doctor, you can get out of anything!"

Interrupting, "Momma, Momma, you are rambling!"

"Baby, I am sorry, you know how I get all worked up sometimes."

"You sound like you need to be behind a pulpit."

"Boy, you know how I am about them women in them pulpits. I live by every word in the Bible and—"

"Ma, you are doing it again. Do you even remember what you were talking about?" Hubert asked.

His mother laughed. "Yeah, boy, we were talking about you and that wife of yours. Hubert, you messed this one up, but you are not the first one to mess up like this, and I am pretty sure that you are not going to be the last. And by accepting Jesus, God forgives you of everything that you done wrong. There may be repercussions, but he forgives you. And once we work on you, we will work on her forgiveness. I know that it is going to be hard for her, and even if you guys split forever she still needs to learn how to forgive, or she will be bitter for the rest of her life trying to figure out and understand why she is not happy."

Months would go by and Hubert would continue to have interviews with different companies. He would continue to have to explain why he resigned. Some jobs he was overqualified for and others just did not pay enough. He contemplated leaving the state, but he did not want to leave his daughter. Hubert was amazed that the job market was as tight as it was for someone with a college degree and experience. On the other hand, he knew that his situation was very unique. He and Shayla would still speak occasionally, but she was still not forgiving him. She was still living with her parents and working at one of the local schools. Hubert was not depressed but experiencing a major change in lifestyle that could lead to depression.

9

Bad Decision

Finding Out about Donovan

Late one evening, Hubert stopped off at Donovan's spot for a drink before he went home. Eric and Clayton had had the same idea and were already there with a pitcher of beer on the table, so he figured that he would join them for a few minutes.

"You guys waiting for girls?" Hubert asked.

"Naw, player, pull up a chair," Eric said, getting up. "I'll get you a glass."

"Hold on, E. First of all, what are you guys drinking?"

Eric looked back at Hubert, as if he should have known what they were drinking. "A pitcher of Bud, what else?"

Hubert called Eric back, "That's all right. I'll order a drink when shorty girl comes over."

Clayton looked at Hubert with a disgusted look on his face. "What, Budweiser is too cheap for your blood? What do you want, Heineken, Corona, or some Dom P?"

Hubert smiled with a look on his face as if he wanted to snatch Clayton in the collar, but before he had the chance, he noticed Donovan walking out of the stockroom with another familiar face, but he could not remember where he knew the guy from. He laid his finger on his forehead thinking, and suddenly it came to him, and he said aloud, "Trunk Clancy!"

"What?" Eric and Clayton yelled out at the same time.

"That guy that Donovan is over there with, I went to school with him. Yes, I am certain that that is who he is."

"What kind of name is Trunk?" Clayton asked.

"His name is Steven Clancy, and he was the biggest troublemaker in school—hell, the biggest troublemaker in town. When he was young, rumor has it, that when he would do something wrong, his father would lock him in a trunk in the basement for hours, so we used to call him Trunk in school, and as we got older, he started answering to the name," Hubert explained.

"So is he really all that bad, or is it that you just don't like him, because I know you can be that way for no real reason," Clayton said with a smile on his face.

Hubert continued to stare at Donovan and his old classmate, not paying attention to the end of Clayton's comments. "No, he is bad news, very bad news. Always packed a gun or a knife. In high school he was on the backseat of the driver's education car with an instructor, and another student was driving, and he saw someone he had beef with in the street, and this cat actually pulled his gun out and shot at the guy six times from the backseat of the driver's education car, but he missed."

"Are you serious?" Eric asked shaking his head in disbelief.

"I am as serious as I look. The student and the driver's education teacher needed counseling, and Trunk was tried as an adult and went to prison, and this is the first time I have seen him since then."

"So did you guys get along?" Eric wondered.

"We knew each other from classes, but I played sports, and he did who knows what. We never had a problem with each other or anything like that. I was not scared of him or anything like that. I guess we never really came in contact."

"Yeah, right, you know you were scared," yelled Clayton, laughing, reaching to give Eric a high five.

Hubert looked at Clayton, and shook his head, and started pushing his chair back toward the table. "I think I will take my drink at the bar." He took about two steps, and looked back at the table. "You know what, E, you need to keep your boy in check before someone else does it. I'll get with you later."

As Hubert walked over toward the bar and closer to Donovan and his new acquaintance, the two noticed Hubert, and Donovan smiled while Trunk pointed at Hubert as if he was saying *I know that guy*. Donovan then threw his hand up to Hubert, signaling him to come over.

Hubert walked over to the two, wondering why his best friend would possibly be talking to a known criminal, and a crazy one at that.

As he got closer, Trunk was the first one to reach out and greet him. He gave him the handshake-hug, like one did as boys.

"What's up, athlete? Long time, right?"

Still in the hug, Hubert looked over his shoulder at Donovan with a very curious look in his eyes. "Yeah, you're about right. It has to have been about five to ten."

"About that," Trunk answered, shaking his head, and licking his lips.

"What have you been up to?"

"Trying to stay out of trouble, while still making ends meet."

"So how are you making out?"

"I have been out of the cell for about two years now, and I must say, I think I do all right for myself. What do you think, D?" Trunk asked looking over at Donovan.

"What are you doing now, if you don't mind me asking?" Hubert questioned again, still wondering why and how Donovan and Trunk knew each other.

"Well, I invest in different things," Trunk answered.

Trunk paused as if he was finished, but Hubert gestured for him to continue talking or at least say something more to make these "investments" sound legit. Hubert knew that Trunk had been bad news from day one, and this was one of those guys that society could not change. In Hubert's mind, he thought that Trunk would either die by lethal injection, or live the rest of his life in prison, or run one of the biggest illegal schemes known to man. So what was he doing with Donovan? Hubert was determined to get some answers before he left. And just when Trunk was about to try and explain, Donovan jumped in.

"We met at a seafood fair on Southside, and I was telling him that I ran a restaurant, and I wanted a new vendor and he was telling me how he knew a guy that could get me some mad prices on seafood, and good deals on a lot of other stuff I could use. So we have been scratching each other's back here and there for a few months now."

"So what have you been up to all these years?" Trunk asked. "I figured your ass would be playing something in the pros."

"I have been living and learning, Trunk, lately more learning," responded Hubert.

"Well, I guess that can be a good thing, but look"—looking down at his watch, reaching out his hand to shake Hubert's and then Donovan's—"I got to break camp. Nice seeing you, athlete. D, hit me up when you get a chance so we can go over some numbers." Trunk then walked out.

"Numbers?" Hubert asked. "Man, what are you doing with that cat? He is nothing but trouble and has a way to pull down everyone around him."

"Well, I don't know how he used to be back then, but all I know is that he has been helping me with people that I need to know, and saving me some change, so I am good with him for now. Besides, man, he served his time, and deserves an opportunity to get back in society. Enough about him. What's your story, what do you have going on?"

Hubert too looked down at his watch, and said, "Look, I have to dip too, but holla at ya, boy, when you get some free time." Hubert gave Donovan a hug and pound, and walked out, waving the peace sign at Clayton and Eric, who were still sitting at their table.

Hubert went home and started going through the mail. He took a look at all of the bills and tossed them on the table, and covered his face and leaned back on the couch. He was not concerned with most of the bills, but the one that bothered him was the fact that he was behind on the mortgage. The letter demanded a payment to get current or they would start with the foreclosure procedure. Hubert lay back in deep contemplation for about forty-five seconds. His phone then went off, and he quickly sat up and grabbed it. It was Donovan.

"What's up, Hue?"

"Chilling and drowning at the same time," Hubert answered.

"What's wrong now, my man, you sound depressed?"

"A brother is struggling with these bills and, man, I mean struggling! Between you and me, I just got a letter talking about foreclosure proceedings on the crib, D," Hubert explained.

"What are you doing right now?"

"What do you mean?" asked Hubert.

"I mean, what are you doing right now?" repeated Donovan.

"Nothing, man, absolutely nothing," Hubert replied.

"Come back to the club."

"Now?"

"Hue, stop asking questions and meet me at the club!"

Quiet and curious, Hubert answered, "I'll be there in a few."

No sooner had he placed the phone back down on the table than it was going off again. He looked at the phone and saw that it was Shayla calling, the very last person he wanted to talk to right then. Still, he knew that they needed to talk.

"Hello."

"Hello, Hue, how are you?"

"I am good, and yourself?"

"I am fine," she answered and then there was a pause for a few seconds. "Hubert, what are you going to do about this mortgage?"

"What do you mean?"

"Stop it, Hue, I called the mortgage company. What were you going to do, let the house foreclose and then tell me?"

"I am going to fix it, just give me some time."

"Like you fixed everything else, your job, your other bills, our freaking marriage," Shayla said, raising her voice towards the end of the statement.

"You left!" Hubert yelled out.

"Did I have any other choice, Hue? Did I?"

Hubert did not answer and they were silent for a while until Hubert asked, "In all of your bitterness, which I understand, do you ever miss me, honestly? Do you ever think about how good we were together? The playing, the laughing, the lovemaking? Do you ever miss me, baby?"

"Why are you doing this, Hubert?"

"Because I know that I miss you. I also know that I was stupid and I know that I done some trying things, but I did love you and I still do."

"Hubert, I am going to answer your question, and then I am going to get off the phone." She paused for a second. "Do I miss you? No, I do not miss you."

Hubert's facial expression completely changed, as she continued.

"I miss the man I thought I married, I miss the man I thought was in a covenant relationship with me, I miss the ambitious family-oriented man I thought that I would grow old with. And, Hue, I wish you had met him, maybe you could have learned a few things from him. I have to go, bye," and she immediately ended the call.

Hubert shook his head, knowing that she was right about everything she said. He wondered if salvaging his marriage—or even a relationship—with Shayla was ever going to be possible or just a hopeless thought.

On his way to Donovan's, he was thinking that Donovan was going to talk with Adrian, and they were going to loan him some money. When he got to the shop, he was shocked to see that Donovan was again mingling with Trunk. Trunk was actually sitting in Donovan's chair in the office.

"I see you again, Alexander," Trunk said.

Hubert reached out and shook Trunk's hand, but was looking over at Donovan for an explanation.

"How are you feeling, Hue?"

"I don't know yet. I'm wondering what type of party we have going on up in here for real," Hubert replied.

"Sit down, my friend," Donovan instructed. "Would you like a drink?"

"No, I'm good."

"Hue, you have two options. You can listen and help us out while in turn we help you out. The other option is you can listen and just walk out. No harm done, no worries. But I have to know that I can trust you before I tell you anything else. What do you think?"

"You know that you can trust me, man," Hubert said to Donovan, looking over at Trunk.

Donovan also looked over at Trunk for the go-ahead. Trunk, rubbing his hands together, nodded his head for him to continue.

"Here's the deal, simple, specific, and without too much information. And, Hue, you know that I would not have gotten you involved if I did not think that it was to help you with your situation as well as mine. So, are you ready for your task?"

"Go ahead, man."

"Hue, there is a car that you are going to pick up on Tuesday. We will give you the keys and the time of the pickup. You are to drive the car to Florida to a designated spot, which is subject to change. And a guy's going to come and ask you to open the trunk. He will remove two tires from the trunk, and replace them with two other tires. You will then drive the car back and place it in another designated area, which is subject to change. You will have all of the necessary information at the appropriate times. After this task is complete, you will return the keys to one of us, and receive in cash $7,500. What do you think?"

"Wow," Hubert said, shaking his head. "What's in the tires?"

"Does it matter?" Trunk yelled out. "Either you in or you out, athlete."

Hubert looked at Donovan in disbelief. "Are you serious?"

"Hue, you need the money, I am just trying to help a brother out," Donovan replied.

Hubert thought about it for a minute, and also thought about his situation, and quickly responded, "I'll do it."

"Bet," Trunk responded, shaking his head. "Now the drop-off joints in Florida are all repair shops, so don't go there getting all Shaggy from Scooby Doo on me. It is going to be just fine."

"Just let me know. You said Tuesday, right?" Hubert asked.

"Tuesday morning," Trunk said, nodding.

"I got you. That will give me three days to set up some payment arrangements for later that week. Yo, I appreciate this, because I really do need it," added Hubert.

"Look, Don," said Trunk, standing up. "I really have to dip. I'll hit you Monday before you start up." Trunk then looked over at Hubert, smiling. "Never thought we would be teaming up, did you, athlete?" He pointed at Hubert. "Drop off, pick up, and you're the man. I'm out."

Trunk walked out, leaving Hubert and Donovan alone. The two tried to avoid eye contact. They were both silent until Hubert broke the ice and asked, "How long have you been doing this, man?"

"Hue, promise me something."

"What's that?"

"No questions. No one knows, man, but no questions."

"All right, have it your way."

"Adrian does not have a clue, and the money helps. I have a nice nest egg that she does not even know about, and when we finally get married, we will live the good life."

"Donovan, you are living the good life now. I actually thought I was coming over here and getting a loan, but you got me stepping to the bad side," responded Hubert, smiling.

"It might seem like we are living the good life to you, but I want more. I want the yacht, the beach house. I want better, Hue."

Hubert, scratching his head, says, "I am going to get out of here and meditate on what just took place."

Donovan called out as he was walking away, "Hue, if you're scared, say you're scared."

Hubert stopped and turned and faced him. "I lost my wife and my job. Am I scared of losing anything else? I need this. I'm good." Hubert walked out pondering about what he had just gotten himself into.

On Hubert's way home, he decided to call Shayla, just to see if she would answer.

"Hubert, why are you calling me this late at night?" Shayla said.

"Whatever happened to hello?" Hubert asked sarcastically.

"Hubert, what do you want now, I am tired," Shayla said in a whiny voice as if she had been trying to sleep.

"Baby, I just wanted to hear your voice."

Shayla paused because she did not have a negative comeback prepared, and because Hubert sounded so sincere. She covered her mouth, and in a cracking voice, said, "Good night, Hubert Alexander, go to sleep." She then lay back on the bed and smiled, remembering the good old days.

Hubert was sensing some breakthrough based on Shayla's attitude, which he thought was encouraging. He was also excited about being able to get some of his finances straight. He was nervous about the trip to Florida but figured that the drop-off should be pretty simple. Hubert was convinced that something illegal was in the tires to be swapped out. More than likely, it was drugs, but he really needed the money.

That Tuesday came, and he received his instructions from Donovan. He made the trip down to Florida and returned back without a hitch. He was amazed at how simple it was. Donovan gave him the money he promised, and Hubert was able to work on getting his bills straight.

10

Conversation Observed by the Wrong Person

Hubert remembered that he had promised Adrian he would go by the uniform store and pay for Nikki's school uniforms. Hubert figured he would call Shayla while he was on his way, to let her know that he had caught the mortgage up.

"Hello," Shayla answered.

"Hey, Shay, how are you?" Hubert asked in a monotonous voice.

"I am okay, what's wrong with you?" Shayla asked.

"Nothing, why do you ask?"

"Because you sound all depressed, Hubert."

"I'm good. I just wanted to call you and let you know that all the bills are current right now. I got it straight."

"What did you do?"

"I got it straight, baby."

"Did one of your little girlfriends give you the money, Hue," Shayla asked.

Hubert became a little agitated by that remark, but held his cool. "Shay, I have not been with anyone since the incident."

Shayla got quiet for a few seconds and then asked, "And why is that, Hue, because you can't wine them and dine them before you sleep with them, because you don't have a job?"

Hubert raised his voice as he answered her. "No, Shay, my head is so screwed up right now with everything going on." Then he got quiet again. "The only one thing that I know is that I know I want you to come home, baby. I want us to work on something. We are just idle right now, and I do not want to be one of those guys in a marriage telling people we do not live together but there is no separation paperwork, nor is there divorce paperwork. We have to move in some direction, and I want you to move home. I am so sorry, baby, please give me another chance?"

Again Shayla went quiet for about ten seconds, then quickly responded, "Hue, I got to go." She then ended the conversation. Hubert shook his head in frustration as he pulled into the uniform store.

As he approached the counter in the store, he told the store clerk that he wanted to pay for Monique Alexander's school uniforms, and that her mother would be in later to pick them up. The clerk looked up her order, and gave Hubert the prices. Hubert wrote out a check, and proceeded to leave.

On his way out of the store, he bumped into Adrian coming in to pick up the uniforms.

"Hey, stranger," said Adrian as she gave Hubert a hug and a kiss on the cheek. "How've you been?"

"Striving and surviving I guess, how about yourself?"

"I am all right."

Adrian looked steadily into Hubert's eyes. She evidently saw what she thought was pain and frustration. She stared a little longer and began to speak again. "Hue, we have been the best of friends for as long as I can remember. You know me and, yes, I know you. You have been avoiding me for months. I am going to pick these uniforms up. Do not go anywhere, I want to talk to you."

Adrian held one finger up to signal that she would be back in one minute, and then she yelled from the counter, "You are not going to leave, are you?"

"I will be right here," Hubert answered, shaking his head.

"You had better be," she said as she was going through her purse, pulling the ticket out for the uniforms. Hubert held the door open for her on her way out with the school clothes.

"I will take those for you," suggested Hubert as he took the clothes out of Adrian's hand.

"Always the gentleman," said Adrian, smiling.

"That's all I know to do."

Adrian smiled and mumbled as if she wanted to say something else.

"What!" Hubert said.

She just smiled and said nothing, and they both started walking toward the parking lot in between the uniform store and a hotel.

"I'm parked over here," she said as she pulled out the car remote and popped the trunk open.

As Hubert placed the clothes in the trunk, he asked, "How is Nikki, anyway?"

"She is good, worried about her father who does not call like he used to, and get this," she added, "the last few times you had her, your eleven year old said that you seemed a little distant."

Hubert shook his head, smiling. "That's your daughter."

Hubert closed the trunk, and Adrian then leaned on the back of the car, looked seriously into Hubert's face and asked, "On a serious note, how are you really doing, Hue, and be honest with me?"

Knowing his relationship with Adrian and their long history, Hubert knew that she was about to pull something out of him. It was something about them; he could never really lie to Adrian. That was the reason he had been avoiding her for so long. He looked down at the ground and back up at Adrian, twice, as if he were going to say something. At this point Hubert's emotions were getting the best of him. He wanted to say Shayla's name, but just stopped. He was hurting so bad that he did not want to talk. If he did talk, he would not even know where to start.

As he stared at Adrian, tears slowly began to fall from his eyes. For the first time since the life-changing fiasco had taken place, Hubert had broken. Adrian and Hubert had been friends for a long time, and this was a side of Hubert that she had yet to experience. Adrian, like most women in this situation, embraced Hubert, and began crying herself.

"I am so sorry," Hubert said, barely getting the words out. "I've messed up so many other people's lives."

Adrian, still speechless and in tears, reached in her purse and pulled out tissues and began to wipe the tears from Hubert's face; but by that point she needed the tissue just as much as Hubert did.

"I have been so selfish," Hubert started, but was quickly interrupted by Adrian.

"Baby, you know that I love you, but you have been selfish since the day I met you almost twenty years ago." She went on to explain, "Hue, that is a part of your character. You possess a self-confident spirit that makes people like you. They like you because you do what you do with so much respect. I hated you for what you did to Shayla, and I am still mad at you. She did not deserve that. You cheated with a married woman, you jeopardized your marriage, her marriage, and now our daughter is confused."

Hubert tried to talk, but had no opportunity.

"No, Hue, let me finish," Adrian said, a little louder, caught up in the conversation. "Now, Hue"—with three fingers up—"that is three families that you have completely screwed up, all for a few funky minutes of pleasure. I know that saying, that if you make your bed you have to sleep in it. No one ever said that you, Hubert Alexander, have to keep your head buried under the covers. That is not going to change anything. You are not the first to cheat, and I am pretty sure that you will not be the last. Hue, you have to assess and address the situation at hand, and move ahead. If you continue beating yourself up, eventually you are going to really hurt yourself. Now we have both cried and wiped our tears, now let's move on, man!" She pushed Hubert in the chest as if to motivate him.

After a sniffle, Hubert asked, "You always knew how to put me in my place, huh?"

"That's what friends do," she added with a cheesy smile on her face. "There is nothing that we can do to change the past. We can only accept our mistakes and make the necessary adjustments for the present and future."

With both of his thumbs, Hubert massaged his temples with his eyes closed. "That is easier said than done."

Adrian looked up in the air as if thinking, and then, raising one finger, began to elaborate on her thoughts. "Remember when we were about fifteen—or sixteen, I guess? I had come over to your house for something. Back then you thought that you had the sexiest body of any teenage male on the planet."

Hubert smiled and added, "Yeah, I was a legend in my own time."

Quickly Adrian added, "Yeah, and in your own mind. But as I was saying, I had come over, and I guess you were just getting out of the shower. You walked through the living room with just the towel on. I am pretty sure that you were trying to impress me, even though I knew that you had shorts on under the towel."

Hubert twisted his lips, and tilted his head wanting to say *Girl, please*, but she continued.

"No, let me finish. Your mother looked at your back and yelled out." Adrian tried to impersonate Hubert's mother. "Hubert, Hubert, boy, what's that on your back? Jesus, boy, you missed your back."

Hubert looked uninterested in the story as Adrian grabbed him by the arm, still laughing and hoping that he did not walk away.

"Wait, Hue"—still laughing—"she came out there with a wet washcloth and some soap, and begins scrubbing your back in front of me. I remember you saying, Momma, Momma, it is not dirt, it happened when I fell from the tree years ago. And your mother"—still laughing—"was so determined, she told you, Boy, that ain't nothing a little Ajax won't take off." Adrian just laughed while Hubert continued to stare at her, without any hint of a smile on his face.

"But, Hue," she explained, "embarrassed as you were right then, you quickly assessed the situation and moved on like nothing ever happened. That is what I have watched you do for years. Even though this is of a much higher magnitude, the same principles apply."

Hubert smiled, shaking his head. "I guess you are right. I did not need the reminder of the Ajax story, but I did need a good lesson from a good friend. Thank you."

"That's what I'm here for."

Hubert and Adrian shared another hug and Hubert started to walk away. He stopped halfway to his truck and turned to Adrian, and asked he walked back toward her. "I know that we done it and all, and Nikki is here, but why is it that we never pursued a more intimate relationship as adults?"

"First of all," she said jokingly, "I only did it with you because I felt sorry for your dirty back." After a small laugh, she paused to gather her thoughts and then went on to explain. "Hue, everyone you knew growing up, your family, your friends, and the people you dealt with back then were dogs, and they had such an influence on you. I knew that if we pursued a deeper relationship, even after I got pregnant, it would jeopardize the relationship we already had. And I did not want to lose you and end up hating you. We already had a pretty strange relationship as it was. So I figure that this was another experience where we had to assess the situation and move on, and I think that it worked out great." She then opened both of her hands as if to say *There it is.*

Seemingly amazed by her response, Hubert nodded his head in agreement. "You are a great friend, a great mother, and Donovan is a lucky man. Thanks again."

Adrian blushed. "You are welcome. And if we were together-together, you would probably have a tag on your toe by now. Take care of yourself, Hubert Alexander."

Hubert laughed, and added, "I really need you to talk to Shay. I will do whatever it takes to get her back."

"You did not hear it from me, but you are getting somewhere. Just do not give up."

"I just want her to say 'I forgive you,' so I know that there is a chance for us." He turned to walk away and told her, "Kiss my little lady for me, and tell her that Daddy loves her, and will see her next Friday at five."

"Make it six thirty if you can. Hair appointment."

"Six thirty it is."

They both got into their vehicles, waved and departed their separate ways. Normally a conversation like this, with a good friends, good advice, and good laughs, would lead to the start of someone moving in the right direction. Unfortunately, this conversation was a little different. Unbeknownst to Hubert and Adrian, while they were talking in between the hotel and the uniform store, the infamous Clayton "C-Nice" Lewis had driven by not once, not twice, but three times. How bad could a person's luck be?

Clayton immediately grabbed his cell phone and called Eric. Eric did not answer, but Clayton was so excited with the information that he waited for the voice mail so he could leave a message. "Yo, E, hit me back, man. I got some mess to tell you about your boy Alexander. Man, you are going to wild out. Call me back as soon as you get this message, out."

He then boldly decided to drive to Donovan's club. Donovan was working in the bar's storage room stacking boxes of wine from a shipment. Clayton did not see him when he walked in. So he asked for Donovan and the hostess pointed him to where he was.

Clayton walked back to him with a very serious look on his face. Now, Hubert had already warned Donovan about Clayton. And Donovan had witnessed Clayton's outbursts at the round table. Still, Hubert told him that Clayton was trouble and that he was an instigator that liked to keep things going. So Donovan looked at him trying to prepare himself for whatever was coming.

"What's up, man?" Clayton asked.

"Working hard, my man. What's the deal?"

Clayton paused for a minute scratching his head, deciding how he would go starting this conversation.

"What, man?" Donovan asked, placing a box on the shelf, and looking at Clayton with his arms opened wide. "I am busy, what is going on?"

"I do not know how to tell you this, man," Clayton responded shaking his head.

"Tell me what?"

"It's about Adrian and your boy Hue."

"What?" Donovan stopped what he was doing, walked over to Clayton with a mean but curious look on his face. "Let's go into my office."

Donovan walked out of the storage room and told one of his workers that he would be in his office and not to be disturbed.

As they walked into Donovan's office, Clayton noticed all of the sports paraphernalia and pictures on the wall, and jokingly asked, "You wouldn't happen to like sports, would you?"

Without a smile on his face, Donovan replied, "Man, you are really trying me!" He got face to face with Clayton and slowly asked, "What do you have to tell me?"

So Clayton sat in a chair and began telling his story. "I was leaving early to go and pick up this outfit to wear to take out this shorty that I met last week." Then he paused and thought. "Or was it week before last?"

"Get back to the story, C!"

"Well, I was driving by that hotel over there on the east end, and man, I saw Alexander and your girl Adrian all hugged up in front of the hotel. I am sorry, man. Alexander is a dirty dude and can't be trusted. I keep trying to tell my boy EP that, but no, he wants to place him on some pedestal. But yo, your boy is foul. But on the real, I could never see myself dating a joint that my boy has a kid by anyway. Man, you always thinking in the back on your mind, are there still feelings there? And that is so apparent in your situation. Man, if I were you—"

"Shut up and get out," Donovan said, interrupting him.

"I feel you, man, I would be upset too," Clayton added, standing up. "But I thought that a brother should know. And I know that it was not mistaking identity or anything like that. I rode by three times, and I know his truck. And your girl has on a purple dress or skirt, with a black jacket. I know what I am talking about."

Calmly, Donovan looked at Clayton. "I want you to leave right now. One more word, and I am throwing you out."

Clayton walked out of the office not saying another word, and left the club. On his way to the car, his cell phone went off. It was Eric, and he quickly answered the phone. "Yo," he quickly responded, "where you been, man?"

"I have been working. What's going on?"

"Man, remember how I told you that you needed to watch your boy Alexander?" Clayton asked.

"C-Nice, I do not have time for this. What do you want to tell me about Hue?" Eric responded.

"I caught your boy red-handed, and get this"—he paused—"with Donovan's girl."

"Man, get out of here, no way."

"EP, I seen it with my own eye, and I did not just see it one time, not two times, but three times. So what do you have to say about that?"

"Wow. So, what, have been stalking him or something, how do you see him three times?" Eric asked.

"See, there you go defending him already. No, I was just out and about to pick up some gear to take out that shorty I told you I met awhile back, and I ride by the hotel, and lo and behold, what do I see, but your boy all hugged up on Donovan's joint. And I thought to myself, for your benefit, this could not be, so I rode by slowly two more times. I know that it was them, but I needed confirmation. I watched both of them get into their cars and everything. I almost ran into another car looking back. So what do you have to say about your boy now?"

"Clayton, I cannot believe this. There must be an explanation, so I am not going to jump to any conclusions until I talk to him about it. So if you do not mind, let me talk to him about it first before you go running off at the mouth like we know you will. I would hate for it to get back to Donovan if it is a complete misunderstanding."

"Too late."

"What do you mean, too late?" Eric asked.

"Man, I am so tired of people always running around here like their mess don't stink when they are doing more dirty stuff then we are. So, man, I told Donovan."

"You got to be freaking kidding me, C. You are not that stupid. Are you that much of a hater that you would run another man down just because people like him more than they like you? Man, you may have started World War

Three, and there could have been a simpler solution. Do not tell anybody that you told me. I am not in it. I am not going to talk to Hue, and I am not going to talk to Donovan until this mess cools down. Man, you are stupid," Eric said, extremely upset with Clayton.

"I don't care, man, I am going out on my date with my shorty. It is what it is."

11

Donovan's Meeting with Feds

Extremely upset about the information he just received, Donovan was puzzled about what his next move would be. Should he confront Hubert, a trusted friend for years? Should he confront Adrian, the love of his life, with whom he planned to spend the rest of that life with? Or should he just not pay any attention to Clayton, knowing that he had a reputation for being a fanatical hater and loved to instigate? Donovan sat shaking his head, thinking this could not be true. But at the same time, thoughts of Hubert's player character and his dealings with women ran though his head. Not only did that fact bother him but also the simple fact that they, Hubert and Adrian, had been together before, and Nikki was the product of that. As his mind wandered, he decided he needed a drink, and being he was the only person left in the club, he reached into his desk, and pulled out his personal stash along with a shot glass. He poured a drink, held the shot glass up as if he were going to toast. He watched the glass for about five seconds, and then swallowed the shot. He then placed the glass and bottle back into his desk, grabbed his keys, and headed out. As he walked out of his office, he was met by two men in nice suits.

"Sorry, gentlemen. The club has been closed for over an hour now," stated Donovan.

"Donovan Price?" one of the men asked.

"Yes, and…?"

Both men flashed a badge before Donovan's face. "Agent Parker, and this is Agent Jacobson. We are from the narcotics division of the FBI," one of the agents explained.

"And what do you want with me?" Donovan uttered nervously, still trying to maintain a calm disposition.

"Mr. Price, I just want to let you know that you are not under arrest or anything as of yet, but we would like to ask you a few questions if you will cooperate," one of the agents advised.

"Do I have to come downtown?"

"No, Mr. Price, we can talk right here if this is all right with you?"

Donovan directed the man to a table in the bar area. "I am sorry that all of my help is gone for the night, but can I fix you guys a drink."

"No, sir, but thanks," one of the agents responded.

The three sat at the table, and one of the agents began talking. "Again, Mr. Price, you are not currently under arrest, but at any time you feel you would rather have an attorney present, even though it would change our entire scenario, let us know."

"What do you mean?" Donovan questioned with his palms starting to get sweaty.

"Mr. Price," the other agent began. "Steven Clancy, a.k.a. Trunk, a.k.a. Troublemaker, has been on our radar for months. We know shipping dates, shipping times, and we definitely know that you are involved. He always orders a rental car, and he only stops at certain auto-parts stores with garages. What we do not know is what he is shipping. So, Mr. Price, I am going to level with you. We talked to Clancy before we talked to you."

Donovan's eyes grew to the size of fifty-cent pieces, but he still said nothing.

The agent continued, "Clancy's pitch was that neither of you were the big man in the picture. He claims that he would give me the name of the big man after he talks with you. Now we do not trust him as far as we can flip him. However we did give him forty-eight hours to talk to you and give us some names, or we are taking you both in. If we have to figure out a charge on the way to the precinct, we will. Then, Mr. Price, you will have no other choice but to obtain an attorney. And let me make you completely aware that we have men watching Clancy's every move like a hawk, and we will do the same with you if necessary. This is as simple as you make it. Give us our man and it is business as usual for you." The two men stood up, and the same agent affirmed, "Forty-eight hours."

"So I am free to go?" Donovan asked.

One of the agents looked back at Donovan and insisted, "Yes, you are free to go for now, but I would consider being more careful about the friends you choose."

Donovan stood at the door and watched the agents as they got into their car and drove off. He immediately reached for his cell phone in his pocket and called Trunk.

"Yo," Donovan said as soon as Trunk answered the phone. "What are we going to do, man?"

"Calm down, playa, relax, we have forty-eight hours to come up with someone. Worst case scenario, we both have to dip in two days."

"Dip!" Donovan yelled. "Man, I have a family and a business. I cannot just dip!"

"Look, D—"

Trunk was about to explain when Adrian was on Donovan's other line. With all the other things going on, Donovan had completely forgotten about the Hubert-Adrian ordeal until this call reminded him.

"Hold on, man, I have to take this call, it's my girl." He switched over. "Hello."

"Hey, baby, are you still at the club?"

"Yes, why?" Donovan answered in a snappy tone.

"God, what's wrong with you?" Adrian asked.

"Just got a lot on my mind, that's all."

"Well, I didn't have anything to do with it, so you don't have to bite my head off," Adrian insisted.

Donovan said nothing even though there were a lot of things he wanted to say. So Adrian went on.

"What time are you coming home anyway? Nikki has been in bed for hours. We could have had a chill night together. I have a surprise waiting for you when you get here."

Now Donovan could only think of what Clayton had told him earlier. With a look of frustration on his face he told Adrian, "Look, I have someone on the other line, I will see you in about fifteen minutes."

In a joking manner, Adrian responded, "But I don't want to get off the phone with you yet. And who are you talking to this late anyway? Is it Hue? It had better be Hue." Then she got quiet, and in a soft, sexy voice whispered, "Come home, baby, I'm lonely."

"I have to go, but I will be there soon," Donovan said as he resumed his conversation with Trunk. "Hello."

"Damn, man, I thought you forgot I was on the other line. Fool, I almost fell asleep waiting on you."

"So what are we going to do, man?" Donovan pleaded. "I can't go to jail."

"Yo, what are you doing early in the morning?" Trunk asked.

"Nothing, I guess. Why?"

"How early can you meet me at your office?"

"Five thirty, six," Donovan replied.

"Naw, man, I did not mean that early! Maybe eight thirty or nine. I would rather talk face to face. People like trying to tap phones looking for information, and as long as we do nothing wrong, we'll have a few drinks in the morning and be laughing about this mess by the afternoon. So go home to your girl. Get you some rest, or do what ya'll do in the middle of the night, and meet me at your spot in the morning. Are you cool with that?"

"I got you, man, and I am cool."

"All right, I am going to bed. Peace."

When Donovan finally made it home, he quietly walked upstairs. Adrian was still lying on her stomach on top of the covers in a sexy, pink negligee. So, like the average man would, Donovan climbed on top of her and started kissing on her back.

"Hey, Meanie," she said as she turned and looked up at Donovan. "I shouldn't give you any. You're lucky I'm still horny. Oh yeah, this is what I wanted to show you."

She then opened her arms, so he could get a good look at the sexy negligee. The two started passionately making out. Donovan then went and locked the door just in case Nikki got out of bed. As he was closing the door and on his way back to bed, Adrian made a statement that killed the entire mood.

"By the way, baby," she asked, "is Hue going to be all right? I worry about him sometimes."

Donovan had now gone from enticed to enraged. He was so furious that he did not know what to say, but she could see it on his face that he was extremely upset. He just held on to the door for a few seconds. All he could think about was Clayton's comments.

Adrian could not see Donovan and asked, "What are you doing, baby?"

Completely livid, Donovan just blew up and in a loud voice shouted, "No, Adrian, what are *you* doing?"

Adrian sat up on the bed and turned the light on, staring at Donovan. "Donny, you are scaring me, what's wrong?"

Still shouting Donovan asked, "What's wrong, Adrian? What's wrong?"

"You are going to wake Nikki up. Are you drunk or something?"

"No, Adrian, I am not drunk. I had a few drinks, but I am not drunk. But let me tell you what I am. I am furious! I am standing here completely turned on by you. I am here in my boxers, you in your lingerie. We are about to get intimate, and you have the audacity to"—in a loud voice—"ask about your baby's daddy!"

"Wow," Adrian responded with both hands over her mouth. "I have never heard you call him that." She paused for a second to get her thoughts in order, as he looked at her in complete anger. "First of all, Donovan, I love you, and I will never love a man, nor do I want to ever love a man the way that I love you. Second, yes, Hubert is my baby's daddy as you want to call him, and I have known him all my life. He is a good father, a good person, and I care about him as a friend, and I thought you did too. Third, I am sorry that I ruined your mood tonight, I did not think asking about our friend would do that. And fourth and lastly, Donovan, I do not know what is going on with you right now, but you are right about one thing, the mood is completely ruined. On top of that, you have never raised your voice at me like this before. So here's the deal"—as she picked up his pants and threw them to him, she grabbed a robe—"You can have the bed tonight. I am sleeping in the guest bedroom." She walked by him, and looked directly in his face, and asked him, "And you ask me why I do not want to get married. We can talk in the morning. But right now Donovan, you"—with all seriousness on her face—"you can go to hell!" She then stomped out of the room and into one of the spare bedrooms.

The next morning Donovan would leave the house even before Adrian could get out of bed. He knew that he had a lot bigger situation to deal with. The first thing he did was to call Trunk to see if he was up, and told him to come to the club as soon as he could because he was already there. He then tried to call a florist to send roses to his house for Adrian, but when he did not get through he changed his mind.

Trunk eventually arrived, getting out of his car looking suspiciously around the parking lot. As he walked into the club, he went into the office not saying a word, looking under the tables, the lamps, and window sill. He then signaled Donovan to walk out of the office.

"Man, what are you doing?" Donovan asks.

"Yo, when you are dealing with the feds, you always have to check for wires and stuff like that. As a matter of fact, you are my boy and all, but can you pull your shirt up? I can't trust anyone right now."

Donovan looked at Trunk like he was crazy, but went ahead and pulled his shirt up. Trunk actually walked over to Donovan and frisked him.

"I'm sorry, brother, I have to be sure," Trunk explained. "So is it all right if we sit at the bar and talk?"

"Sure," Donovan answered looking at Trunk strangely.

"And what are you calling me for this early for anyway? Didn't I say eight thirty?"

"Man, it is almost eight thirty now," Donovan replied, looking at his watch.

"Yo, I have been in and out of the joint for years, and I ain't trying to go back. So peep this, I have been thinking hard all night. We need to figure out who we can pawn this thing off on, right? The feds have too much information, but I do have an option, I just don't know how you are going to feel about it." Trunk got quiet for a moment, and stared at Donovan.

"And?" Donovan asked insistently.

"Yo, Donovan, you are my man, and I want you to think long and hard about this."

"What, man?"

"You say that you don't want to go to prison, right?"

"Right," Donovan answered quickly, "I   "

Trunk interrupted and asked him again. "You say you do not want to go to prison, right?"

"No," Donovan yelled out. "Who does, and where are you going with this, man?"

Trunks paused for a moment, and then asked, "Is it too early for a drink around this place?"

Walking behind the bar, Donovan said, "You start talking, I'll pour the drink." Donovan pulled two glasses, and fixed a drink for the both of them. Meanwhile, Trunk did not say a word until Donovan placed the drinks on the table, so Donovan was now in greater suspense. "Say what you have to say, man, I'm ready!"

Taking a sip from the glass, Trunk asked, "How close are you and your boy?"

"Who?" Donovan responded quickly.

"How close are you and your boy Alexander?"

"Why?" Donovan responded curiously.

"Yo, D, I am going to ask you the question one more time. How close are you and your boy?"

Donovan also took a sip from his glass, and was reminded of Hubert's supposed actions with Adrian, and replied, "We're all right, college friends, that's it." Suddenly it clicked in his head where Trunk was going with the conversation. "No, man, I can't set him up!"

"Yo, listen for a second. Think about this before you respond so quickly. Let me make my point, then I'll finish my drink, leave, and you can hit me back later. Can you at least listen to what I am proposing?"

"I can't sell nobody out, man, but make your point"

"Here's the deal. I am a businessman, you're a businessman, right?"

Donovan nodded wondering where this conversation was going.

Trunk continued, "The last I checked, isn't your boy unemployed? And if my memory serves me correctly, aren't you raising his daughter anyhow? So I know that it seems wrong from the start, but who has the most to lose? I am going to be as honest as I can be with you, playa, if I go down, you're coming down too! So we set your boy up as the mastermind, he gets hit with the federal kingpin statute, and we will both walk, probably not even have to take the stand. So my real question to you is who do you want to raise the girl and your family?"

"This is crazy, how are we going to make all of this happen?" Donovan asked curiously.

"Yo, that's simple. We set him up with another run, a bigger run. This time we offer him more money, give him an advance so he has lots of cash on him, and ask him to drive his own vehicle. At some point we let the feds know where and when he is leaving. Donovan, I know that it's your boy and all, but it can be as easy as it sounds. The other consequence is we all get locked up, and Alexander may not, being he was just the driver. All you have to do is make the call big-time. I am going to dip for a while. Think about it and hit me on my cell, and I will come back with more information. Do not talk too much over the phone."

Donovan just stared at Trunk. In his mind he was wondering, could he actually do this to Hubert? At the same time, he was wondering how Hubert could have done him so wrong. Donovan was in deep thought, and Trunk watched him as he seemed to be going into a daze.

"Yo, you all right?" Trunk asked. "You seem like you need to go back to sleep or something."

Donovan nodded his head, and then spoke, "No need for you to leave, I am in. Just give me the details, but, Trunk, after this, I am out, done!"

"Bet, I am with that," Trunk answered, rubbing his hands together, smiling. "Although we still have some loose financial ends to tie up. I do have to talk to a few more people, so we will be on the same page. I will be back in about three hours."

Donovan walked Trunk to the door, and they exchanged a hug and pound, and as Trunk walked out, he added, "Do me a favor, have your boy meet us here around noon. This will all be over in a few days, playa."

Trunk drove off, and Donovan contemplated on whether he would call Hubert or Adrian first. Even though he did not want to talk to Hubert, he knew he had to do what he had to do.

"My man," Hubert said, answering the phone.

"You sound like you were wide awake."

"I think that I am going to surprise Shay later this morning. I am going to head up and just stop off at the school unannounced and ask her to go to lunch. What's the worst that could happen? So I have been up cleaning, because I am going to beg and plead for her to come home. What do you think?"

The entire time that Hubert was talking, Donovan could only think about Hubert and Adrian. "I think that it is a good idea, but can you postpone it for another day, for a friend?"

"What's the deal?" Hubert asked curiously.

"Can you meet us at the club at noon instead?"

"Meet you and who?"

"Trunk. I promise you it will be really worth your while." Knowing Hubert and Shayla's situation, Donovan felt like he had Hubert against the ropes, so he continued. "You do this deal, with a few slight changes, then surprise Shay, and with the money, you will be able to treat her like a queen. She will definitely take you back then."

Hubert thought about it for a minute, and quickly decided. "You know what, you are right. I will be there at twelve."

12

The Setup

Hubert would make it to Donovan's club at about 12:15 p.m. Donovan and Trunk were already there patiently waiting for him. As he walked in, both Donovan and Trunk looked down at their watches. Hubert paid them no attention.

"Same deal as last time, right?" Hubert asked.

"Same deal," responded Donovan. "Are you straight with it?"

Trunk leaned forward and looked at him. "You're not getting nervous on me, are you, athlete?"

"I'm good, Trunk, just making sure that everything is still the same."

"Now the drop-off is a little different, but, as we told you the last time, it is for a quick in-and-out transaction with the least amount of trail that can be followed. Drop the product, get the cheddar, and get back to your fam. You still got one of those, don't you? Ladies' man like you," Trunk added laughing, looking over at Donovan.

Hubert smiled and looked at Trunk, and then at Donovan, and replied, "Yes, I have a family. And for the record, I appreciate you guys helping me with my finances, but this is going to be my last drop. When I think about what I am actually doing, I think about all the things that could go wrong. I have too much going on in my life right now to add a criminal record. So I am going to get you straight this time, but this is it, and you know that your secret is cool with me."

Trunk nodded his head and said, "That's good. Do it this time, and we'll get you straight." Trunk spoke in a tone as if he were doing Hubert a favor.

"What time do I pick up the car?" Hubert asked.

"Remember I told you that there would be a slight change of plans this trip," Donovan said.

Hubert nodded his head.

"Well, Hue," Donovan said and paused for a few seconds. "Can you drive your truck?"

"No," Hubert shouted before Donovan could even get the words truck out of his mouth. He stared at Donovan, and replied, "Hell no!"

Donovan and Trunk looked at each other, thinking of what to say next. Then Trunk took center stage in the conversation.

"Look, athlete, here is where we stand. The rental company was starting to ask too many questions, and was also cutting into our profit." He then walked around to

Hubert, and placed his arm around his shoulders. "How about this. Drive your truck and we will give you an extra $3,500 up front. Think about it, $3,500." Rubbing his hands together and smiling. "That's November's house and truck note on top of everything else. Your percentage in this thing is steady growing, baby. Look, think about it for a few hours then get back to one of us for further instructions."

Hubert sat down in a chair, shaking his head in deep thought, knowing that most of what Trunk said was true. But the risk was so much greater using his personal vehicle. He also thought that if he could address his financial problems, things would be easier dealing with Shayla in the hope of her eventually returning home. This dilemma played on his emotions so much that he started sweating.

"Are you good, man? Do we need to give you a minute, or do we need to give you some water and a towel?" Donovan asked, smiling.

Hubert thought for a minute and then threw his hands up in the air in surrender. "All right, I don't need a few hours to think about it, I'll drive my truck."

"Are you sure?" Donovan asked, looking out the corner of his eyes at Trunk.

"My man!" Trunk called out. "You won't regret it, I promise you."

"Man, I am regretting it right now, but a man's got to do what a man's got to do. Man, I need something to drink."

"Get the man a drink, Donovan, to calm his nerves," Trunks said, smiling. "Now when you get on the road, don't be looking all nervous like you do right now, because the police are just going to stop you for looking suspicious."

"I am good man. I just want to get this mess over with so that I can start getting my life in order."

Donovan's poured the three of them a drink and then held up his own glass for a toast. "To getting life back in order."

Hubert and Trunk repeated, looking at each other, and the three enjoyed the drink and a laugh.

"Look, Donovan, I have to break camp, but I will get with the both of you before the night is out." Trunk looked over at Hubert, reaching out to shake his hand. "You're the man, player, I will holla back at you later. I'm out." Trunk finished his drink and walked out.

Donovan and Hubert were both quiet for a few minutes, when Hubert asked, "Hey, do you want to shoot a game of pool?"

"Yeah, I will dust you off right quick."

The two went to the pool table and Donovan started racking the balls.

"Why are you racking?" asked Hubert.

"Since the loser has to rack I figured that I would be courteous and rack up the first one, being I have no intentions of losing any." Donovan smiled, looking up a

Hubert as he positioned the balls in the triangle. "I did not want you complaining that you were racking too much."

As the two started the game, Hubert asked, "So how are things at home?"

Donovan tried to act like he did not hear him, focusing on his shot, but he did look up at Hubert after making the shot, and Hubert asked again.

"So how are things at home?"

"They are good, why do you ask?" Donovan answered staring into Hubert's eyes.

"Things are so quiet. I was just making small talk, if that is all right with you," Hubert responded.

Donovan did not reply, but continued to shoot. Hubert could see that Donovan was a little preoccupied, so he tried to avoid asking any more questions. Donovan missed his shot, and looked over at Hubert and said nothing but "Your shot."

As Hubert was shooting, Donovan then asked out of curiosity, "So have you found a job yet?"

"Man, if I found a job, do you think that I would be making this run? Man, it is hard out there. The competition is overwhelming, everything is so job specific. You are either overqualified, or they are not paying you what you are worth, or they do not offer you one benefit. Others say they are just experiencing a hiring freeze. I never thought it would be this hard to get a job."

"Hue, you have to start somewhere," said Donovan.

After shaking his head because he missed a shot, Hubert looked at Donovan and paused for a second. "You know, that is the easiest statement for someone to say who has a job. The reason why some people further their education and get degrees is so they do not have to flip burgers and sweep floors with hopes of one day being the store manager."

"I feel you, man, but still—"

"But still what?" Hubert interrupted.

"Sometimes a man has got to do what a man has got to do. Your options are limited right now. That is why I say that you have to start from somewhere. I am not trying to be defensive or anything. I am just stating the facts," Donovan explains.

The two continued to shoot with no conversation other than calling their shots in the pool game. That is until they were both on the eight ball, when Hubert was taking the shot for the win. He looked down at the shot, mentally calculated, then called a shot.

"Side pocket."

Donovan hunched his shoulders as if to say he did not care.

Hubert then dropped the stick on the table, but before taking the shot he looked at Donovan. "Look, man, we have been boys for a while, and I can tell if something is wrong. Man, you are the closest friend that I have. You have been with me through the thick and the thin, the good and the bad. I love you like a brother and I do not know what to think about this recent attitude of yours. Maybe I am reading it wrong, and I apologize if I am, but you know that I am straight up and that I am going to say what is on my mind. If I done something wrong to you, by all means, let me know. Friends should be able to do that, right?" Hubert asked.

"We're good, man. Take the shot," Donovan said with a serious look on his face.

"Donovan, this is what I am talking about, right there. Man, we are boys, we never used to be like this. I remember introducing you to Adrian years ago."

"Look," Donovan said, raising his voice some. "I do not want you to bring her name up! Please take the shot, man."

Just then Donovan's phone went off. He looked at his phone and placed a finger in the air for Hubert to hold on. It was Trunk. "What's the deal, Clancy?"

"All is good, are you still with your boy?

"Yeah, we are shooting a few games of pool."

"Well, here is the deal. You are going to meet me today, and I am going to give you the package and three tires that need to be changed, and your boy is going to pick it up from your place. Listen, I know that tomorrow is Saturday, but it has to jump off tomorrow evening. When Alexander is on the way, you text me and I will make some calls, and it is going to go down right after that. Bet?" Trunk asked.

"Bet," Donovan responded, looked over at Hubert.

"All right, hit me when you are on your way, and let us get this monkey off our backs."

"I got you. I will give you a call when I am on my way. Out," Donovan added as he ended his phone conversation. He then looked over at Hubert. "Are you going to take your shot?

Hubert took the shot and won the game, and as he was waiting for Donovan to rack, he noticed that Donovan was putting the balls away.

"We done?" asked Hubert.

"Slight change of plans. I am to go and meet Trunk, and pick up the packages. You are to come to my house and pick them up from me when I call you tomorrow, so that we can stay exactly on schedule. This works out fine, being this is not your weekend with Nikki. So I am going to have to run, and we will pick this back up another day."

"What about our conversation?"

"We're good, just do not be late when I call you, and gas up."

"I will not be late, you know I am never late. I think that I am going to talk to this crazy wife of mine and tell her that I am going out of town, but that when I get home we really need to meet and talk. Wish me well, man, I really need to know where we are headed. So let me get out of here."

"All right, I will call you later and let you know what's up," Donovan replied.

The two exchanged a hug and pound, and as Hubert was walking out, he turned to Donovan and said, "I meant what I said, you are like a brother to me."

On his way back home, knowing that he had a successful way of getting his financial life back in order, Hubert thought about calling Shayla. He grabbed his phone, scrolled down to her phone number, where the name still read *the wifey*. But he paused for a few seconds wondering what moods she would be in or if she would even answer the phone, knowing it was him. So he decided to call his mother first.

"Hello, God bless you," she answered.

"Hey, Ma."

"Hey, son, how are you? I have been worrying about you. I have not heard from you in a while. A couple of the sisters and I from the church have been praying for you. Yeah, for you finding a job, your finances, and even for God to heal your marriage. Yeah, Sister Anita, Sister Lynn, and you know Linda, don't you? That's the one—?"

"Ma!" Hubert yelled out interrupting her sentence.

"What, Hue?"

"How *are* you? Gracious," he said implying that she was talking too much.

"Oh baby, I am good. You know how I can get rambling sometimes and can't stop. How are you anyway?" his mother asked.

"I am good too, just trying to get some things straight financially. By the way, have you heard from Shayla lately?"

His mother did not respond.

"Ma, did you hear me?"

"Hold on, boy, I am thinking. Yeah, she called last Wednesday, right before Bible study, because that is what prompted me to get with the sisters and pray for you guys. Yep, it was on Wednesday, last Wednesday. Why, when was the last time that you talked to her?" his mother asked.

"A few days ago, I think. She used to be so mean on the phone, I should have stopped calling."

"Boy, I know that I raised you better than that. Who messed up, Hue?"

"What do you mean?"

"Hubert Alexander, you know exactly what I mean. Who messed your marriage up?"

"I did, Ma, but where are you going with this," Hubert said softly.

"Let me explain something to you, Hubert."

Hubert interrupted her. "Ma, I am driving."

"Well, keep your eyes on the road and listen. My Bible tells me that when a man chooses a woman, he chooses a good thing. I could be wrong, but I do not know of any translation that says 'when a woman chooses a man.' So, Hubert, did you choose her?"

"Yes, ma'am, I chose her."

"So let me get this right, and you hear me out. Pull over if you have to. You are telling me that you chose to take this woman from her mother and her father's care, where she seemed to be doing just fine, if I can recall correctly? Wait, don't interrupt yet. You then became her provider, taking the place of her parents and starting a life where you are now the man of her house. Now you stop me if I am wrong about anything I say. You then allowed the devil to infiltrate you and assist you in making stupid and selfish mistakes which had drastic consequences, which greatly affected both of your lives. Guess what, Hubert, you are still that man that not only chose her but stood in front of God and many others and promised to provide, love, honor, and cherish her. The question is, are you man enough to fight for what you want? Or did you just waste years of a young woman's life because you thought that you were grown and could handle the pressure of wearing the big-man pants? Hubert, you and your uncles used to take so much pride in saying that they were great because they were an Alexander. You are an Alexander, Hue, what are you going to do?"

"She won't talk to me about us, Ma, she barely answers my calls."

"Hubert, you hurt her dearly, what do you expect? But I know that Shayla still loves you. Do you still love your wife?"

"Yes, I do."

"Do you want to work at saving your marriage?

"Yes, I do."

"Hubert, you are at a point where you must be willing to accept some nos to get to some yeses. You call and call and you call. You keep telling her that you love her even if she says that she hates you. When you eventually get your foot in the door, keep showing her how much you want to make up for what you messed up. Show her more love than you have ever shown in your entire life, and see what happens. Most importantly, Hubert, apologize to her and ask for her forgiveness, and then go to God and ask for his. I am telling you what will work. It will take time and a lot of work. Let God lead you, son. So many marriages fail because it is so easy give up, but fight for what you chose. Are you still there?"

"Yes, I am still here," Hubert answered. "All of that sounds good and made a lot of sense, Mom, and I am going to try. And Mom, I asked her for forgiveness, but she changes the subject or ends the conversation. She does seems like she is coming along real slow, and I am excited about that, but she needs to tell me something. Don't I at least deserve that? And you know that I do not have that relationship that you have with God."

"Well, do you believe in him?"

"Yes, I do believe in him, but I am not ready to change some of the things in my life yet, to truly commit to him. I will one day, but I am just not ready yet."

"Hubert, he changes your life when you commit to him. If we could control and change it when we wanted to, why would we even need him?"

"I guess that makes sense. So I am going to call her, and try everything that you said. And, Mom, it was great advice. Thanks. Look, tomorrow, I am going to run down to Florida to check out this insurance job."

"In Florida, and on a Saturday. What kind of job is that?"

Hubert, quick on his feet, responded, "Florida is the home office, and they are having a conference, and they just wanted me to ride down and observe, to see if I was really interested."

"Okay, son, you be careful. And I am always praying for you, you need to consider praying for yourself. Now let me go now, and start cooking. I hope to see you Sunday."

"Love you, Mom," Hubert said as they ended their call.

By that time Hubert had made it home and was sitting out in the truck in his driveway. He got out of the truck, went into the house, and sat on the couch, preparing himself for the call with Shayla. He grabbed his phone, and thought to himself, *Here goes nothing.*

The phone rang about four times on her end, and as Hubert was thinking about what kind of message he would leave, Shayla picked up and answered.

"Hello."

"Hey, how are you?"

"I am okay, and you?"

"I am making it, I guess."

The conversation went quiet for a few seconds, when Shayla asked, "Hue, what do you want?"

"For starters, I was calling to say that I love you, and that I miss you, and that I want you to come home. I am going to work on getting all of our finances straight, but I care about you more than I care about those finances. Money is slowly getting better, and I think that our relationship is also getting somewhat better. I just need you closer to me. You can sleep in the spare bedroom, or I will sleep in the spare bedroom. But I need you near me, baby."

"Where are you getting this money from? What did you do, rob a bank?"

"No, I have a friend moving some money around for me that was left in my retirement."

"Oh, that is good, but I thought you took all the money from your 401(k)."

"No, I took a loan out on it."

"You said for starters. What else is there?" Shayla asked almost impatiently.

"Well," Hubert said then paused.

"Well what, Hue?"

"Shayla, I know that I really messed up, and I hear it from everyone and anyone who knows us. But I miss you, I miss us."

"Look, Hue, I have to go."

"No, Shay, please do not hang up, just listen."

"Five minutes, Hue, then I have to go."

"As I was saying, I know that I messed up, but just hear me out. I have no excuse, I was a complete idiot, and I took advantage of one of the greatest gifts ever given to me. I took you for granted, and I did not respect our vows. Shay, I lost so much thanks to my foolishness, but you are the only thing that I really miss. I am not me without you, and have not been myself since you left. I have no excuses, I have lost self-respect and my dignity. I can start gaining it back with you accepting my apology and us starting from somewhere. Shayla Alexander, do you forgive me?"

Shayla did not say a word. Hubert just held the phone, waiting to hear something. He even looked at the phone to make sure that he hadn't hung up on her.

Then she very softly said, "Hubert, I will think about it."

"Thanks, Shay, that answer is good enough for me. I love you, baby," Hubert answered excitedly.

"Bye, Hubert."

Hubert went back out to the truck, and took the picture off the seat, the picture he had taken months earlier off of the wall. He walked back into the house, smiling, looking at the picture. He then placed the picture back on the wall in its original location. He stepped back to make sure the picture was centered and then he just shook his head, smiling, thinking that things were about to be better. Hubert thought to himself that that moment on the phone had been the most reassuring moment he had had since the disaster on the job.

No sooner had Shayla ended the call than she had another coming through. It was Hubert's mother.

"Hi, Mrs. Alexander, how are you?" Shayla asked puzzled, looking at the time.

"God bless you, baby, I am good. How are you?"

"I am doing fine," Shayla responded.

"No, baby, how are you really doing? You and I have not had a decent talk since you left Hue. Now tell me, how are you doing?"

Shayla paused because she did not know exactly how she wanted to answer the question. "Mrs. Alexander, no disrespect to you, but I left Hubert for a reason. I needed time to think and reevaluate my life. I did not want to talk to you because I did not want you trying to force me to make a decision."

"Shay, I cannot force you to make any decision. God is ultimately in charge of any decision we make. I love my son, and I love you as my daughter. I also know that Hue still loves you," Mrs. Alexander said convincingly.

"Well, he had a funny way of showing it back then," Shayla said, raising her voice a little.

"Now he realizes that he made an enormous mistake that has affected all of our lives. Baby, sometimes in our lives we get so caught up in our accomplishments and successes that we forget who got us there. We become so vain and cocky. Can I say that word?" Mrs. Alexander said, thinking she said something wrong.

Shayla laughed. "You're all right."

Mrs. Alexander continued, "But they become so vain, and full of themselves, they think that everything is about them. Hubert lost control of who he was, and the devil took over. And with the devil taking over, Hue was out of control, and God had to bring him down, baby."

"Look, Mrs. Alexander, I clearly understand where you are coming from. Unfortunately, I am placing the blame on Hubert, because he made those choices. Now he is blowing my phone up, writing letters and sending e-mails, like I have to take him back. He should have thought about our marriage when he made those choices."

"Shayla, do you still love him?"

"With all of my heart, and I am never going to stop loving him. That does not mean that I just forgive him and we move on like nothing ever happened. I will not be hurt like that ever again. So I need time, regardless of him begging and pleading like he has lost all of his pride."

Mrs. Alexander got quiet on the phone for a few seconds before she went on talking. "Pride. I am glad that you said that word. That is Hue's problem, and it was also his father's problem. I would tell him that it is all right to be confident, but God does not like it when you are so proud. I remember when Hue was going to college and working to pay that child support. He doesn't think that I know, but he would be so broke that he would never have enough gas to get home the day before payday. His check would clear at nine p.m., so he would go as far as he could, normally that grocery store. But he would go there at five p.m. when he got off, and would stay there until nine p.m. so that he could get money out of the ATM for food and gas. Baby, he would do this just because he was too proud to ask anyone for money. Now when you tell me that he is begging and pleading like he has lost his pride, I know that something in Hue has changed. Does that make any sense?"

"It makes a lot of sense, but it does not make the pain go away, Mrs. Alexander."

"Baby, nothing is going to make that pain go away but the healing power in your heart that comes from God. Let me ask you a question. Do you pray?" Mrs. Alexander asked.

"Probably not as often as I should, but I pray in the shower, I pray when I am alone in the car driving, I pray when—"

Mrs. Alexander quickly interrupted her. "Stop, stop, stop! Baby, that is praying, but you need some intimate prayer with God. You are praying and you are taking a shower, making sure everything is clean. You are praying and you are driving, making sure that no one runs you off the road, or that you do not run any one off the road. Baby, if you were making love to a man, and he also wanted to look at the game on ESPN during your lovemaking, how intimate would that be?"

"I guess I never looked at it that way," Shayla answered.

"Baby, you have to find that secret place where it is only you and God, where you can cry and make all of the ugly faces that you want. Do not shortchange God. He is not a God of shared capacity. He is a jealous God. I am not telling you to stop praying in the shower or on the road, but you need to find that secret place with no interruptions and let God have his way with you, baby. Now, I didn't lost track of what we were talking about. What were we talking about, baby?" Mrs. Alexander asked laughing.

Shayla, also laughing, answered, "Hubert's pride and my prayers, ma'am."

"Well, I am going to say this one last thing, then I am going to bed, because I am getting tired and losing my train of thought. Help me, Jesus! Maybe I will say more than one thing and get off, I am going to say three. First of all, I love you and you are so special to me. Second, Hubert really does love you. And lastly, baby, I do not think that Hue is much concerned with you jumping back into his life right now but he is more focused on receiving your forgiveness. Well, I said my piece, and I am going to bed. Good night and God bless you, baby. Allow him to lead and guide you through tonight, tomorrow, and forever. May heaven continue to shine upon you, and grace and mercy be with you in all that you do." Mrs. Alexander then hung the phone up without giving Shayla an opportunity to say goodnight, or to even respond.

Shayla replaced the phone, laughed, and said to herself, "Hubert did say that she could talk." She then lay on her bed, staring at a wallet-size picture of her and Hubert. Shayla thought about the content of the conversations with Hubert and Mrs. Alexander, until she eventually fell asleep.

13

Worst Possible Outcome

Hubert woke up early that Saturday morning feeling like he was about to have a burden lifted off his shoulders. The first thing that he wanted to do was to call Shayla, but he thought it would be a better idea if he waited until he returned. She said that she would think about it, so he did not want to push it. That was enough for him. He had so much energy that morning; he swept, mopped, vacuumed, and even washed a load of clothes. He wanted to make sure that the house looked spotless if Shayla was to return. Hubert had done so much housework that by noon he was tired. Hubert took a shower and afterward figured he would squeeze in a quick nap before the long drive.

Hubert woke up around 2:00 p.m., called Donovan and told him that he was on his way. He packed a bag, just in case he had to stay later, and proceeded to head over to Donovan's. Upon arriving to Donovan's home, he noticed that Adrian's car was not there. As Hubert was getting out of his truck, Donovan was already out and headed to his own. Donovan looked at Hubert, signaling him to come over and give him a hand. Donovan had three tires in the back of his SUV.

"What's up, bro?" Hubert asked. "Where are the girls?"

"They stepped out for a minute, but they will be back. Can you grab one of these?"

Hubert looked at the tire wondering, *How did they stuff anything in a tire?* But when he picked up the tire and noticed the weight, he knew that there was something in there other than air. "Man, this tire is heavy, how do—?"

Donovan quickly interrupted him. "Remember, no questions about what you are carrying."

Hubert, laughing at Donovan being so serious, saluted him, saying, "Aye, aye, captain."

The two loaded the tires into the back of Hubert's truck. Donovan walked to his truck once again and returned, this time with a package. He handed it to Hubert. "This is the little bonus we talked about."

Hubert took the money, smiled, and threw it on the backseat. "They know that I am coming, right?" asked Hubert.

"It will work out the exact same way it did last time, Huey. Stop worrying, player. By this time tomorrow, we will be sitting back drinking cold Coronas or Heineken as we count all that extra change we made," said Donovan.

"I hope you're right," Hubert said very quietly.

"Look, man. Since we met, haven't I always had your back?" asked Donovan.

Hubert quickly responded, "Naw, kid, I think that that is vice versa."

"Well, you are probably right," Donovan said, smiling, "but did I not have your back the last time you needed me?"

"Yeah, but it was me that was taking a chance," explained Hubert.

"Yeah, I guess you are right again. But I got you this time, Hue. Now get out of here, because you are running out of time," Donovan said as he leaned forward to shake Hubert's hand.

"I will call you when the mission is accomplished," Hubert told Donovan.

Donovan did not respond right away, he just stared into Hubert's eyes as if he were starting to get worried himself.

"Did you hear me, man?" Hubert asked.

"Huh?" said Donovan, coming out of his daze.

"I said I will call you when the mission is accomplished," repeated Hubert.

"No! Do not use the phones until I call you, okay? Whatever you do, do not forget that," said Donovan, still seeming a little nervous. "Now you need to get on out of here, Hue."

As Hubert was beginning to get into his truck, Donovan walked over, and as he hugged him he seemed to get a little emotional, saying, "Thank you for this, man. I love you, and be careful out there."

"I got this," Hubert replied. "Just don't forget to call me, because I might end up in the Bahamas somewhere sipping on gin and juice." Hubert then got into the truck and drove off, waving the peace sign.

Now, at the exact same time that the cops were closing in on Hubert's tail, Adrian had returned home to find Donovan sitting on the step with both hands on his face. They still had not spoken since the other night.

"What's wrong with you?" Adrian asked.

"Nothing at all," Donovan responded.

Adrian and Nikki walked by to go into the house. "Nikki go ahead in, I will be in there in a minute." And she returned and sat down beside Donovan. "I do not know what is going on with you. Maybe I shouldn't have said Hue's name and I am sorry. It is just that…" She paused.

Donovan looked over at her. "It is just that what?"

Adrian went on. "Earlier on that same day that we argued, I saw Hue."

"Seen him where?"

"At the uniform store. He paid for Nikki's uniform and I picked them up," said Adrian.

"What uniform store?"

"The uniform store out there right beside that nasty hotel. I do not know what you and Hue talk about, but Don, he was hurting so much. He was so upset about Shay and everyone's life that he messed. He started crying, I started crying, and we just had a moment, and that is the only reason why I asked about him that night."

While Adrian was talking, Donovan had started sweating and trembling, realizing what he had done. Adrian did not realize what was happening with Donovan because she was too busy talking at the time.

She continued, "Baby, I love you, and I do not like fighting with you. I think my hormones got the best of me that night." She then looked over at Donovan. "Baby, what is wrong?"

Donovan did not have a clue what to say. He could only think that he was sending his best friend and Adrian's daughter's father to jail based on something Clayton the troublemaker told him. He looked at Adrian and told her, "No, I am sorry. I was wrong, and I promise I will make it up to you and Nikki." He then kissed Adrian and hugged her tight. Suddenly, his cell phone went off. Donovan did not even look down at it.

"Aren't you going to get that?" Adrian asked.

Donovan thought that it was Hubert and did not want to take the call, especially with Adrian around. He grabbed his phone, and it was Eric. "EP, what's up?"

"You at the club yet?"

"No, not yet, what's up?"

"I think you need to turn the TV on, man, put it on channel five."

"All right, man, I'm gonna do that right now," Donovan said as he got off the phone and went in.

"What's wrong, baby?" Adrian asked following Donovan in the house.

"I don't know yet. EP told me I needed to put the TV on channel five."

As Donovan turned the television on and changed the station to 5, an anchorwoman announced: "For those of you who are just joining us, the TV 5 chopper was out doing another story when we noticed this high-speed car chase taking place. This is not a recording, this is live. This is happening right now, and we brought it to you first. We will gather as much information as we can as the chase continues."

"Oh my God," Adrian yelled out. "That's Hu!"

Donovan was in shock and just stared at the TV. He shook his head as he watched the chase progress. His phone went off, but it was Trunk, so he figured he was watching it also. In minutes, phone calls went everywhere in that community; everyone that had access to a television was watching the chase. This included Mr. Marshall, Alisha, Clayton, Latrell, and many others. One of the most disturbed viewers was Hubert's mother. She sat watching the television and praying at the same time that it was not her son. But to her dismay, the next thing that the anchorwoman said would confirm who the driver was.

"Again, this is Julie Carpenter, TV 5 News. For those of you who are just joining us, the TV 5 chopper was out doing another story when we noticed this high-speed car chase taking place. This is not a recording, this is live. This is happening right now, and we brought it to you first. And we have an update for you. We are told that this was a joint operation by the FBI, the state, and local police. They are said to be chasing drug kingpin Hubert Alexander. They are going to make an official press conference when the chase finally, and hopefully, comes to a safe ending. We do, however, know that we have one police car that took a tree head-on. We will keep you posted as we find out more information."

Everyone that was watching the news and knew Hubert yelled out "Drug kingpin!" They all knew that the Hubert they knew had no dealings with drugs. This was shocking to everyone. But no one wanted to stop watching.

As the high-speed chase continued, the more times Hubert looked in the rearview mirror, the more police cars he could see joining in, and he seemed to be running out of road. With all of the lights following, it looked like fireworks hooked onto his bumper. Still Hubert would not slow down. In a panic, and scared to death, he began to think.

He thought about how he and his little girl would laugh and play; he thought about his mother always pushing for him to get his life straight with the church. He thought about the sermon he had heard the last time he visited church, and how the minister seemed to be talking directly to him. He thought about all the people he let down in the past, and all the people he had hurt, wondering to himself, what made him into the person he was, and how could he not care about other people's feelings?

Hubert noticed that he even had helicopters over his head. What was he going to do? Thinking he had a little lead, Hubert tried one more back road. As he made the turn, he was just as amazed at how many cars were following him. There was a sharp curb coming up, where the speed limit stated 25 mph. Hubert was going almost 90 mph and tried to make the curb, to no avail. The truck flipped several times before smashing into a tree. Everyone watching covered their mouths and waited as the police, with their guns out, surrounded the truck. They quickly called for an ambulance. The anchorwoman woman would return one more time with the devastating news.

"Again, this is Julie Carpenter, TV 5 News. The high-speed chase has just come to a tragic end. We are told by officials that Hubert Alexander, alleged drug kingpin, was pronounced dead on the scene. Also, Chester Parson, who had been a state police officer for only three years, was also killed, when his car was run off the road by Alexander's car earlier in the chase. We will have a lot more information, including the press conference, tonight at ten. This is Julie Carpenter, TV 5 News, and we bring it to you first."

Everyone was shocked and in disbelief at what had just happened. Adrian crying, with her eyes covered with her hands, continuously screaming *No*. She then turned around, to realize that Nikki had been sitting on the stairs watching the news the entire time with them. Tears rolled profusely down Nikki's face. Adrian ran over to the stairs and they both just cried. Donovan walked into another room, still dazed. He took a seat on the couch. Slowly the tears started rolling down his face, as he asked himself, *What have I done?*

Mrs. Maggie Alexander, Hubert's mother, dropped to her knees and, even in tears, grief, and disappointment, she prayed.

Adrian's cell phone started ringing. Still crying, she looked to see who it was. It was Shayla. Adrian was nervous about answering the phone, because she did not know if Shayla knew. Adrian wiped her eyes and cleared her throat, and answered. "Hello."

"Hey, Adrian, I did not want to call Mrs. Maggie. Is it true?" Shayla asked.

Crying on the phone, Adrian answered, "I am so sorry, Shay, I am so sorry."

"No, Adrian, no. Please, Adrian, no."

"Shay, where are you? Shay, are you there? Shay."

"Adrian, I am on the road. I was going to go to the house and surprise him. He asked me to come home last night. I know that I have been stubborn, but I needed time. And now he's gone," Shayla said, crying.

"Look, where are you right now?" Adrian asked.

"About thirty minutes from your place."

"I know that you may not want to do it, but we have to go over to Mrs. Alexander's, then we have to go and get the body and make arrangements. I am here with you through this whole thing."

"Okay, thanks. Oh my God, how is Nikki?" Shayla asked.

"She is as well as to be expected. I hope that my baby can just cry herself to sleep tonight. And Donovan is in the den. He has not said a word, so I have to let him handle it his way also."

Shayla would make it over to Adrian's and the two would ride over to Hubert's mother's house. They knocked on the door. Mrs. Alexander walked to the door and opened it. From the look on her face, she knew. She reached out and grabbed and hugged Shayla like she never had before. Shayla just cried and cried and cried. Adrian was rubbing Shayla's back, while Mrs. Alexander was praying out loud.

After they all calmed down, Mrs. Alexander took both girls by the hand and said, "I know that we have so many arrangements to see to, but I just want one thing to be known. My boy was a lot of things, but he wasn't no drug dealer."

"We know, let's not worry about that now. Let's just go and get him so he can go home for good," Adrian insisted.

Everyone who ever knew Hubert seemed to have shown up at his funeral. The place was standing room only. The family walked in by the open casket and then to their seats. They kissed him on the forehead, touched him on his hands, or just rubbed their hand along the edge of the casket.

Shayla was the only one to actually stop over the casket for a while. She reached in, and grabbed Hubert's hands. And with tears in her eyes, she looked down at Hubert and tells him, "I never stopped loving you, Huey, and if you are wondering, I forgive you."

She then took her seat, and others followed, viewing the body and taking their seat. All of Hubert's acquaintances were there except Christina, Trunk, and Clayton.

The funeral would proceed as planned. Now it was Pastor Williams's turn. As he stood over the casket at the funeral service, he held one finger in the air and said softly, "If there is a heaven or a hell—an I am pretty certain that there is—based on what I know, I firmly believe that if I died today, there is a place for me in heaven. I believe that with all my heart. And you know what, even if I had doubts about if there was a heaven or hell, I would still live a life acceptable to God, so I would not have to chance it." He paused for a few seconds. "I know that I would go there without a doubt." He then looked out at the church and asked, "How many of you can honestly say that? I know that we call this a home-going service for Brother Alexander, and we have heard all the great things about him, and how he was good people, like one guy said, and would help anyone. But church, did Brother Alexander meet the criteria to make it into heaven? We will never know. But if your number were to be called up tonight, tomorrow, or next week, you have to ask yourself, where would your next home be? Many of you just think you set in the ground and rot, and that is it. What if you are wrong and you get judged based on the lack of knowledge? The Bible says 'My people are destroyed because of the lack of knowledge, because they reject that knowledge.' How about you today? I know that this seems unorthodox to some of you at a funeral, but it has been laid on my heart, as I watch this young man whose life has ended so early and abruptly, to ask that if there is anyone here that would like to accept Jesus as Lord and Savior, would you come now? Play something soft, would you? No one is asking you to stop everything you are doing right now, because if you could stop on your own, you would not need a savior. Amen."

Some of the church shouted *Amen*, as he continued.

"This is you just acknowledging that you believe that Jesus was the Son of God, and that he died on the cross for your sins, and the sins of the world. Will there be one today? I will ask that question that I asked earlier—if you were to die today, tomorrow, or next week, where would your soul go? Where will your eternity be? Will there be one?"

The church was extremely quiet for about ten seconds. Suddenly Eric stood, and slowly walked down to the front of the church with tears in his eyes. Alisha, also teary-eyed, would stand next, and make her way to the front of the church. And next, Donovan and Adrian, holding hands, would accompany the two.

Pastor Williams opened his arms wide, and said, "God bless all of you, you have made the best decision you will ever make in your life." He then again looked at the church and asked, "Will there be one more? Church, do not let that ambulance, that bullet, that disease, or that sickness make the decision for you. Will there be one?"

Very slowly standing from her seat at the front row, with all eyes watching, with tears pouring profusely down her face, was Shayla.

The burial would take place, and Hubert would only be a memory. Life would eventually go back to as normal as possible for everyone else. And each day, the enemy will bring more challenges to each one of them. The ultimate goal in everyone's life should be to clearly understand the reality that you are a sum of your choices.

Afterword

This was a fictional novel with fictional characters and situations. Although fictional, many of us can relate or identify with at least one of the characters, if not all of them. One of my main purposes in writing this story was to influence people to evaluate the decisions that they make in life. If we could learn to contemplate all of the possible results of a simple decision, I think that we would truly be more equipped to make more morally intelligent choices. Unfortunately, many of us today think with instinct instead of insight. Effective decision-making can either strengthen or ruin a family. Some ethical, moral, or emotional decisions we make can impact generations. These decisions, if not properly thought through, can pose a serious threat to your marriage, your money, your family, your friends, your health, and, ultimately, your mind. I like to compare decision-making to those old cartoons that show the angel on one shoulder and the devil on the other, both trying to persuade you one way or another. This is essentially how life is. Many of us take entirely too long comprehending this; that is why we are a sum of our choices. Not to sound too religious, but in the Bible, God told his people: "I have set two choices in front of you: life and death. Choose life." I am a firm believer that when he spoke of death, he was speaking of a spiritual death, where we are in darkness and separated from him. We are all now born in darkness and the only way to receive the light and true insight is through accepting his Son, the Light of the World. And then, with time and every decision you make with Jesus involved in your life, you will understand the responsibilities and consequences of your actions. You may still not always make wise decisions, because sometimes God has your heart but not your head. It is up to you to give that to him. This can be an enormous decision, with great reward or continuous regret. Thank you, and may God bless all of you who took the time to journey with me into the saga of a modern-day Lot.

CPSIA information can be obtained at www.ICGtesting.com
Printed in the USA
BVOW01s0502230916

463049BV00005B/6/P